It was crazy.

Wonderful, but d
She did not even
Quinn was arroga
He obviously cared only about getting what
he wanted when it came to his job, and it was
clear from the grin that he was used to getting
what he wanted from women, as well. He was
precisely the sort of man she disliked.

So how could one kiss from Quinn Sutton have
affected her like that?

How could he have made her feel as if she were
about to fall into an old-fashioned swoon?

Dear Reader,

Welcome to the romantic, thrilling and fast-paced world of Sensation.

This month brings us the second story in the brand-new and exciting ROMANCING THE CROWN series. One book a month for twelve months, where the royal family of Montebello is determined to find their missing heir. But the search for the prince is not without danger—or passion—as you'll see in *The Princess and the Mercenary* from Marilyn Pappano. Look out for *The Disenchanted Duke* next month.

Popular author Carla Cassidy continues THE DELANEY HEIRS with *To Wed and Protect*. Remember to watch out for the next story in May. Another new series to look out for is RaeAnne Thayne's the OUTLAW HARTES where three rugged men find themselves on the right side of the law—and looking for love! *The Valentine Two-Step* kicks us off and the next story—*Taming Jesse James*—is in March.

Finally, the ever-popular Candace Camp brings us *Smooth-Talking Texan*, another story from A LITTLE TOWN IN TEXAS; *Miranda's Viking* by bestselling author Maggie Shayne has an unusual hero who will leave you spellbound; and Linda Randall Wisdom makes sure her story gives us plenty of juicy *Small-Town Secrets*.

Enjoy them all.

Happy Valentine's Day!

The Editors

Smooth-Talking Texan

CANDACE CAMP

SILHOUETTE®
SENSATION™

Silhouette, Silhouette Sensation and Colophon are registered trademarks of Harlequin Books S.A., used under licence.

First published in Great Britain 2003
Silhouette Books, Eton House, 18-24 Paradise Road,
Richmond, Surrey TW9 1SR

© Candace Camp 2002

ISBN 0 373 27223 5

18-0203

Printed and bound in Spain
by Litografía Rosés S.A., Barcelona

CANDACE CAMP

is a *USA Today* bestselling author and former lawyer, is married to a Texan, and they have a daughter who has been bitten by the acting bug. Her family and her writing keep her busy, but when she does have free time, she loves to read. In addition to her contemporary romances, she has written a number of historicals.

Books by Candace Camp for her
A LITTLE TOWN IN TEXAS series

Silhouette Sensation

Hard-Headed Texan
Smooth-Talking Texan

For Pete,
My smooth-talking Texan

Chapter 1

Lisa Mendoza drove to the county courthouse in Angel Eye, ready to do battle. This was the sort of case that she had gone to law school for, a clear miscarriage of justice, an example of prejudice and abuse of power. She felt none of the ambivalence that she often did in the criminal cases she had been assigned so far, where her client was usually clearly guilty and her only hope was of plea-bargaining down to a lesser sentence. Nor was it the small consumer grievance or landlord/tenant dispute that had come to her at the legal aid office since she had moved to the small town of Hammond, Texas. This was an Hispanic teenaged boy held without due cause in a small-town county jail.

She narrowed her eyes and her foot pressed down a little harder on the accelerator as she thought about

it. Less than an hour ago Benny Hernandez's cousin
had sat in her office in Hammond and described to
her how his seventeen-year-old relative had been
stopped the day before by the sheriff and hauled off
to jail even though he had committed nothing more
serious than a traffic violation. The sheriff had not
released him, not even charged him with any crime.
There had been no arraignment, no hearing, and his
large and loving family was understandably worried,
though most of them were too in awe of the Law—
with a capital *L*—to do anything about it. Therefore,
Enrique Garza, the man in her office, had decided to
take it upon himself to hire an attorney for the boy.

"Sometimes Benny can be a little wild," he had
admitted with a deprecating smile, "but he's not a
bad kid. I don't want to see him get hurt."

Lisa could imagine the sheriff she was driving to
see: a middle-aged, potbellied Anglo "good ol'
boy," no doubt, who had judged Benny Hernandez
guilty of some crime simply because his skin was
too dark. *Wasn't Bertram County, of which the little
town of Angel Eye was the county seat, one of those
south Texas counties famous for their politically
powerful and corrupt sheriffs? The kind of county
where the sheriff ruled with an iron fist and took
bribes and routinely brought in the graveyard vote
for the right politicians?* She was almost sure she
remembered reading an article in a Texas magazine
a few years ago about these sheriffs that had ruled
as they pleased earlier in this century. Bertram
County had been one of the counties examined. That

sheriff had died in some sort of scandal some years back, if she remembered correctly, but it would not be unusual for the political machine to continue with another man of the same ilk at the head of it.

The sheriff would be contemptuous of her, she was sure. He would probably take one look at her and write her off as negligible: young, a woman and Hispanic, as well. It would not be the first time someone had done so. But Lisa had learned that being underestimated often worked to her advantage, and she had made certain that a number of men who had done so had soon regretted it. Her lips curved up in a smile as she thought of the coming confrontation. She intended to make sure that Sheriff Sutton would rue the day that he had tangled with her.

Quinn Sutton leaned back in his chair, legs crossed negligently at the ankles and feet propped up on his desk, and sighed. He was bored, and he was frustrated, and for one of the few times since he had moved back to Angel Eye, he wondered if doing so had been the right thing.

One simple investigation…and it had been dragging on for two months now. The guys he had worked with in San Antonio would probably bust a gut laughing if they knew how he was floundering around on this country case.

He had thought he'd caught a break with Benny Hernandez. The kid knew something, he was sure of that, but so far, he had been determinedly silent, and there was only so long he could hold him here, given the flimsy charge he had run him in on.

The sound of voices raised in an outer room stirred him from his reverie. He paused, listening to the heated rise and fall of women's voices, but he could not make out the words. One of the voices was Betty Murdock, his secretary, but he did not recognize the other one. He frowned and started to rise from his seat.

At that moment, Deputy Hargrove stuck his head in the door, his face alight with interest and amusement. "Hey, Sheriff, come out here. You gotta see this. It's that new attorney I told you about."

"Who? What attorney?" Quinn rose to his feet and started toward the door. "Oh, you mean the woman?"

Hargrove nodded. "Yeah. The looker. Remember, I told you about seeing her over at the district courthouse in Hammond last month?"

"Yeah, I remember." The truth was, the memory was faint. Hargrove was usually raving about some girl or the other.

"Well, she's out there giving Betty hell about seeing you."

"Maybe I ought to oblige her then," Quinn said lazily and slid past the deputy into the outer office.

His eyes went across the office to his secretary's desk, where Betty now stood, her face flushed and hands on her hips combatively, facing another woman. He looked past the ample form of his secretary to the other woman, and everything in him went still. Later, he could only describe the feeling, a trifle embarrassedly, as something akin to being hit by a stun gun.

She was not the most beautiful woman he had ever seen. She was not as polished and sleek as Jennifer had been, nor did she possess the icy blond society-princess beauty of his future sister-in-law, Antonia, or the stunning Hollywood good looks of that actress that Jackson had brought to the Fourth of July picnic. But there was something about her that hit him like a fist in the stomach.

She was dressed in a lawyerlike tailored suit, brown with a cream-colored blouse beneath the buttoned jacket, and low-heeled brown pumps. Her makeup and shoulder-length bobbed hair were equally low-key. But the plainness of her clothes could not disguise the fact that her figure was enticingly curved, and the expanse of leg that showed beneath her knee-length skirt was shapely. Her hair, smoothly curved under, was thick, black and lustrous, and her light olive skin and huge brown eyes, ringed by thick black lashes, had little need of makeup. She was vivid, warm, passionate…and in an utter fury about something.

"I insist on seeing Sheriff Sutton!" she snapped, leaning forward pugnaciously toward his secretary. "Whatever wonderfully important thing he's doing, I suggest you go in there and tell him—"

"Why don't you just tell me yourself?" Quinn suggested lightly.

Both women, startled, swiveled to face him.

Lisa was, for the moment, bereft of speech. Sheriff Sutton was, indeed, a prototypical sheriff, but not the middle-aged redneck image she had envisioned. He was, rather, what the State Association of Sheriffs might use as a poster boy. In his early thirties, he was tall, even without the added inches of the cowboy boots on his feet, and his long, lean body and wide shoulders filled out the tan shirt and slacks of the sheriff's uniform to perfection. Lisa was aware, with some surprise—and chagrin—of a deep, primitive thrill of response that snaked down through her abdomen at the sight of him. Nor was it just the muscular set of his body encased in the Western and decidedly masculine uniform that could make a woman's heart beat a little faster. His face was something that drew one's eye.

He was not exactly handsome, though he had even features and a well-cut mouth that stirred another primeval response in Lisa. A scar beside that mouth and the determined set of his jaw gave his face a certain toughness in repose. And when he smiled, as he did now, his mahogany-brown eyes twinkled with an impishness, his mouth quirking in a way that was far too boyish to be termed handsome. What he was, Lisa thought, as he walked toward her now, eyes alight and focused solely on her, was a charmer. She had met other men like him—not many, admittedly, but a few—and though they might not be the best-looking man around or the smartest or the wealthiest, they were invariably devastating to the female sex.

"Sheriff Quinn Sutton," he said now, extending

his hand and smiling into her eyes in a way that said they were the only two people in the room. "Pleased to meet you."

Lisa squared her shoulders. Sheriff Sutton was going to find out that this was one woman who was immune to his charm. "Lisa Mendoza," she replied in a clipped, cool voice and gave his hand a brief shake. "I am Benny Hernandez's attorney."

"Are you now?" Sutton's eyebrows rose in lazy surprise. "Well, that's interesting. I didn't realize he had one."

"Obviously, or I assume you would have chosen someone else to ride roughshod over."

"I beg your pardon?"

"I think you know what I'm talking about," Lisa replied calmly, not fooled by his air of bemusement. "You arrested and are holding my client without any basis. I presume that in the general way you are intelligent enough to find someone without an attorney to protect their rights when you are in the mood for harassing minorities."

The smile left his eyes, and his brows snapped together. "Now just a minute, Ms. Mendoza…"

"I would like to see my client now," Lisa went on, plowing right through his attempt to explain himself.

Anger flashed in his red-brown eyes, and Lisa thought he was about to fire back a response, but he only set his jaw and replied, tight-lipped, "Come with me."

He swung around, strode out of the office and

down the hall without looking back to see if she was
following him. Lisa hurried out the door after him,
determined not to fall behind his long-legged stride.
He led her to the end of the hall and turned down
another corridor, leading her down a set of stairs and
through another institutionally beige hallway or two
before coming to a set of locked metal double doors,
flanked by a window covered with a metal grille. The
uniformed man behind the window looked out at
them.

"Hey, Sheriff," he said in a Texas twang and
reached over to push a button.

There was a loud metallic noise as the doors unlocked, and Sheriff Sutton pushed one of them open
and walked through, holding it open for Lisa.

"Bring Benny down to visitation," he told the
deputy in the small room behind the window, now
looking out at them through a matching window on
this side of the doors.

"Sure thing, Sheriff," the man replied, his eyes
going curiously over to Lisa. Lisa felt sure he was
wondering who she was, but there had been a note
in the sheriff's voice that did not invite questions.

He walked her down a short hallway past closed
doors and ushered her into a small room. There was
little in the room except a cheap metal table in the
center, bolted to the floor, and a chair on either side
of it, also bolted securely to the floor. Lisa set her
briefcase down on the table and turned to face the
door. She wanted to get a good look at her client

when he walked in, alert for any sign of scrapes, cuts or bruises.

Somewhat to her surprise, when the door opened, escorted in by the deputy, the slight teenaged boy dressed in an orange jail jumpsuit was not even wearing manacles. A quick but intent inspection revealed no mark on his pleasant face. His eyes widened a little when he saw her, and he blurted out, "Who are you?"

"I am your attorney, Benny," Lisa told him with a smile, reaching out to shake his hand. "My name is Lisa Mendoza. I'm here to help you."

He looked a little disconcerted but shook her hand tentatively, glancing from her to the sheriff as if for explanation. Sheriff Sutton merely shrugged.

Benny launched into rapid-fire Spanish, and Lisa held up her hands in a stopping gesture.

"Wait. I'm sorry. I—I'm afraid I don't speak Spanish," she told him, her cheeks flaming with embarrassment.

The boy stared at her in some astonishment, and behind her she heard the sheriff let out a guffaw of laughter, quickly stifled. She turned toward him, sending him a furious glance. "I will need a translator, Sheriff."

His eyes danced merrily, and Lisa could feel her blush deepening. Her lack of knowledge of her ancestors' language was embarrassing enough at any time, but it was far worse in front of this man, who she was sure was delighting in her discomfiture.

"Okay," he replied, struggling to keep his lips straight. "I can help you out."

"You?" Her brows soared in surprise. "*You* speak Spanish?"

"Well, yeah," he admitted, the grin twitching back onto his lips. "I was a cop in San Antonio for eight years. It's kind of unavoidable. 'Course, if you'd rather have a native speaker, I can send down Deputy Padilla."

"A law enforcement official would hardly provide the confidentiality that—" Lisa shot back hotly.

"No, hey, that's okay," Benny interrupted pacifically. "I can speak English instead. It's cool."

"Are you sure?" Lisa asked, turning back to look at him. "Because I don't want there to be any misunderstanding or difficulty in communicating with me."

Benny looked faintly affronted. "Sure, I'm sure. I grew up here."

"Of course." Lisa smiled at him apologetically. "I'm sorry. I'm afraid I didn't have time to fully acquaint myself with your history. When your cousin explained your problem to me, I thought it was best to come right over."

"My cousin?" Benny's expression changed to amazement.

"Yes. He hired me on your behalf."

"Julio?" Benny's voice rang with astonishment. "Julio hired you?"

"No. It was Enrique Garza who hired me."

"Oh." Something flickered in Benny's eyes, and

the surprise left his features. "I see." He looked toward the table. "Well, let's sit down."

Lisa followed him to the table and sat down across from him, scooting forward to accommodate the immovable chair. She opened her briefcase and took out a yellow legal pad and pen, laying them on the table. "Now, Mr. Hernandez…"

A faint smile touched the young man's face. "Benny. Everybody calls me Benny."

"All right. Benny. Mr. Garza told me something of your circumstances, but I'd like to hear it from you."

"Hear what?"

"All about what happened when Sheriff Sutton stopped you the other night." She paused and turned her gaze significantly on Sutton, who was still standing a few feet away from them, watching them with narrowed eyes, his arms crossed over his chest. "Sheriff Sutton, it's hardly a confidential talk with my client with you looming over us like that."

He smiled, that same flashing smile of startling charm that he had used earlier in his office, and gave her a slight bow of his head. "Of course, ma'am." She felt sure that if he'd been wearing his sheriff's Stetson, he would have tipped it with old-fashioned courtesy. "The deputy will be right outside the door if you have any trouble." His gaze slid over to Benny, one eyebrow lifting.

"No trouble, Sheriff," Benny said, lifting his hands in an innocent manner.

Sutton nodded and left the room. He paused outside the closed door for a moment, frowning in thought.

"Everything all right, Sheriff?" Jerry asked finally.

Quinn looked at the man and smiled faintly. "I don't know, Jerry." The truth was something felt distinctly wrong, both with the case and with his own internal equilibrium. The arrival of Lisa Mendoza seemed to have thrown them both off.

"You ever hear of a fella named Enrique Garza?" he asked the deputy.

The deputy frowned. "Garza? No, not offhand. There are plenty of Garzas, but I don't recollect an Enrique. Now, there's a guy that works in Meltzer's body shop on First Street who's named Enrique, but I'm pretty sure his last name is Ochoa."

Quinn nodded. "Well, take Benny back to his cell when he's through talking to the lady. I imagine we'll have to release him after that, but I'll give Ms. Mendoza a chance to tell me off first. She looks like she's bustin' to do that. I'll be in my office."

"Sure thing, Sheriff."

Quinn strode back through the maze of hallways and stairs to his office. Most of his staff, he found, were sitting waiting for him in the outer office, faces turned expectantly toward the door. He walked in and raised his eyebrows exaggeratedly.

"What's this? All the crime in this county's been settled? You folks need something more to do?"

With a martyred sigh, his secretary turned back to her desk and the others scattered.

"Say, Ruben…" Quinn stopped him as he walked back toward his desk. "Come into my office."

Ruben followed him and closed the door behind him. "Hargrove's right, for once," he said with a grin, turning to face Quinn. "She is a looker."

"Yeah, she's a looker," Quinn admitted, a faint smile tugging at his lips. "Don't think she's too happy with me at the moment, though."

Ruben grinned with a noticeable lack of sympathy.

"Do you know if Benny has any cousins named Enrique Garza?" he asked the deputy, who had lived all his life in the small town of Angel Eye.

"Garza?" Deputy Padilla looked doubtful. "I don't think Benny's related to any Garzas. 'Course, I don't know that much about his real dad's family. Why?"

"Because that attorney told him that his cousin had hired her, and he looked like he about swallowed his tongue, and he said, 'Julio?'"

"Julio?" Ruben repeated and began to laugh. "Julio Fuentes? My three-year-old's about as likely to find an attorney and hire her as Julio Fuentes."

"That was the impression I got from Benny's expression. But then Ms. Mendoza told him that his cousin Enrique Garza had hired her. Benny recognized the name; I could see that. But he got this funny look on his face… You know anybody at all named that? Related to Benny or not?"

"Off the top of my head, no. But there are lots of Garzas. Could be from Hammond or someplace else, too."

"Yeah. Well, I'm going to call Señora Fuentes and see if she knows who he is and what relation he is to her grandson."

"You think Señora Fuentes knows about that attorney?"

"My guess would be no." Quinn smiled ruefully. "I expect she's going to give me holy hell about letting Benny go, too."

"Better you than me," Ruben replied, grinning. "I used to get enough of that for cutting across her lawn when I was a kid."

"Listen, check around. See if you can find anything out about this guy Garza."

"Sure. You think it's somebody involved in what's going on at old man Rodriguez's place?"

"That'd be my guess."

"You think Ms. Mendoza's connected with them?"

"I don't know." Quinn frowned. "They hired her, if I'm right, but that 'cousin' stuff—I'm guessing she doesn't have a clue what's going on."

Quinn didn't want to admit, even to himself, how intensely he hoped that was true.

"He arrested you because you had a broken taillight?" Lisa asked, amazement sending her voice soaring upward.

"Well, no, not exactly. I mean, that's why he stopped me. Then he looked at my license and walked around the car and all. Asked me questions."

"Questions? About what?"

Benny shrugged, not looking at her. "Oh, you know. Where I been and who I was hanging out with." He raised his eyes to meet hers. "Just general kind of sh—stuff, you know, like cops do. And he said a car like mine had been seen, you know…"

"Seen? What do you mean? Seen where?"

Benny frowned. "I'm not sure. He didn't say exactly. I—he was kinda holding out on me, you know, like, waiting for me to say something I shouldn't."

"Okay. What do you think he was wanting you to say?"

Benny shrugged elaborately. "I don't know."

Lisa had the feeling that her client, if not precisely lying to her, was at least possessed of more knowledge than he was letting on to her. It didn't surprise her. One canon of criminal law that she had had drummed into her in law school was this: *Your client always lies.* She had experienced it herself with her clients, and not only in the criminal cases she had had. All clients wanted to present their best case to their attorney, even if it meant hiding a few things that would later sabotage their case. She wasn't sure how much of it was sheer denial, the hope that if they hid the negative things from their attorney, they wouldn't really exist, and how much of it was the simple human desire to look good in the eyes of their new ally. Whatever it was, it all too often backfired. But no matter how many times she warned them, it was rare that some little lie didn't surface at some point during a case to muddy it up.

She started to press Benny about it but decided to

let it slide. Whatever Benny was concealing, it wasn't really the point. What mattered was that Sheriff Sutton had hauled Benny off to jail.

"So—when you didn't say whatever he was hoping you would say, what happened?"

"Finally he told me he was gonna have to take me down to his office."

"Did he say why?"

Benny shrugged again. "I don't know. 'Cause I wasn't telling him anything."

"Is that what he said? Specifically?"

Benny frowned, concentrating. "I don't remember exactly what he said. I think he said he wanted to ask me some questions, and, oh, yeah, he made me get out of the car, and there was this beer can on the floor, and he picked it up and asked me if I'd been drinking. And I said, no, 'cause I hadn't."

"Did he give you a test? Breathalyzer, walking straight, anything?"

"Nah. He knew I wasn't drunk. Only there was some beer still in the can, see, and so he was saying I was a minor in possession, like that." Benny shrugged. "It wasn't even my beer can. Julio left it in my car the day before, but..."

"So he took you to jail on an MIP—a minor in possession?"

"I guess. I mean, we both knew he was just jacking me." Benny seemed unmoved by the thought—accepting, Lisa assumed, that getting hassled by the law was simply a fact of life.

"Why?"

"I don't know." Benny repeated what seemed to be his favorite phrase, even when offering up what he obviously did know in the next sentence. "'Cause I didn't tell him what he wanted to hear. He wanted to grill me."

"And did he?"

"He took me into his office and asked me a bunch of questions and then he had Padilla lock me up." He grimaced. "Probably hoping I'd tell that *cabron* something just because he's Chicano." He followed this statement with a Spanish word that Lisa did not recognize but the derogatory intent of which was clear.

"And when did this happen?"

"Day before yesterday."

"So you've been here ever since? Were you arraigned? Taken into court for a hearing?"

He shook his head. "I ain't been nowhere but my cell."

"What did he tell you he was charging you with?"

"I don't know. MIP, I guess. He said he was going to let me think about it and then we'd talk some more." His lip curled expressively. "Trying to scare me."

"Did he hit you?" Lisa asked. "Hurt you in any way? Threaten you with bodily harm?"

The teenager looked at her in faint surprise. "Nah. He's not like that. He's okay, most of the time." He paused, then added, "He's just...you know, playing his game. And I'm playing mine."

Lisa sighed. This was not the first time she had

encountered this attitude of being locked with the police in some sort of elaborate game, the rules and movements of which were known to her clients and the cops. Benny had his game face on, the blank mask that withheld emotions, giving nothing away. She had seen it on a hundred faces of young men, black, white, and Latino, when she had worked at the Dallas Public Defenders office the last summer of law school.

"You know, Benny, this is a game where he holds most of the cards," she pointed out. "The best thing for you to do is not play. Just clam up and call for your attorney next time. Will you do that? Will you call me?"

He nodded. "You gonna get me out of here?"

"Yes. When we get through here, I'll have a talk with the sheriff. He knows he doesn't have enough to hold you here. And if he refuses to release you, then I'll get a writ and go to court."

Lisa stood up, picking up the pad on which she had taken a few notes and sticking it back into her briefcase. She shook Benny's hand and went to the door. The deputy opened it and escorted her through the set of locked doors back into the courthouse.

She walked purposefully up the stairs and though the halls, getting lost once, but finding her way back to the wide central hall of the main part of the courthouse. She wondered if the sheriff had led her the most confusing way on purpose.

Her heels clacked briskly on the old granite floors as she headed toward the sheriff's office. She was sure that everyone along the corridor would know that she was coming. She turned into the large outer office, where the secretary and two deputies were at their desks, seemingly busy about tasks, but she could feel their sideways glances as she marched through and into the inner office of the sheriff, not pausing or even glancing at his secretary for permission.

Mindful of the listening ears outside, she closed the door behind her. She didn't want the sheriff's employees to hear what she had to say to him—not out of any concern about embarrassing the sheriff, but because she was well aware that the knowledge that his people were listening would make it harder for the sheriff to back down and might result in his refusing to release Benny simply because of the loss of face.

Quinn Sutton rose from his seat behind the desk. Lisa was reminded all over again of how tall and overwhelmingly masculine the sheriff was. She quelled the involuntary response of her own body to that masculinity.

''Ms. Mendoza.'' Sutton smiled in that cocky way that she found both profoundly irritating and annoyingly charming. ''Have a seat.'' He gestured toward the chair in front of his desk.

''This won't take long.'' Lisa was not about to let her guard down around this man, even to the extent of relaxing enough to sit. ''I just came here to tell you that I want my client released immediately. You know, and I know, that you arrested him on the flimsiest of pretexts and brought him down here, where you have been holding him without arraignment for two days now.''

"Well, yesterday was Sunday," he pointed out, and amusement lit his mahogany-brown eyes.

Lisa's hand clenched tighter around the handle of her briefcase. "Yes, and today was Monday, and you still didn't arraign him. You may find it amusing to hold a young man without reason for the weekend in the county jail, but I can assure you that I do not. First you stop him, no doubt doing a little racial profiling...then—"

Quinn grimaced. "Oh, come on, don't go throwing around your big-city buzzwords in here. There was no racial profiling going on."

"Then," Lisa plowed ahead, ignoring his words, "you harass him, even though he had done nothing except have a broken taillight, making him get out of the car. You find an empty beer can in his car, which you had no right to search—"

"I didn't search," Quinn responded tightly. "It was in plain view on the floor. And it wasn't empty."

"Oh, right," Lisa replied sarcastically. "It had, what, maybe a teaspoon of liquid in it? On the basis of that, you hauled him down to the jail. When was the last time you took a kid to jail for an MIP instead of just writing him a citation?"

"Last weekend," he responded, crossing his arms across his chest. "This isn't the big city, Miss Mendoza, and I take underage drinking seriously. My deputies and I don't write a drunken teenager a citation and turn him loose on the road. I find it's pretty effective with an MIP or DUI to have them come down to the jail and spend a while waiting for their parents to pick them up.''

Lisa hesitated, momentarily nonplussed by his response, then picked up on his last statement. ''Benny Hernandez has been here quite a bit longer than a 'while.' Why weren't his parents called to come pick him up?''

''Because his father skipped out before Benny was born, his mother's in San Antonio living with her new boyfriend and his stepfather's in prison in Huntsville.''

''Oh, I see. That makes Benny automatically a criminal, right? He's got a crummy homelife, so the place for him is jail? His family is bad, so he is, too?'' Lisa's eyes snapped, and her body was stiff with anger.

Quinn Sutton's eyes lit with an answering anger. He was also aware that the emotion in Lisa Mendoza's face had stirred a primitive desire in him that was as strong as his anger. That fact irritated him even more.

''No, Ms. Mendoza,'' he said, his voice clipped and precise. ''As a matter of fact, most of the people in Benny's family aren't bad at all. His mother just has the world's worst choice in men. One of her brothers, his uncle Pablo, has been in and out of jail most of his life, but the other two uncles are as honest and hardworking as anybody in Angel Eye. His grandmother raised Benny most of his life, on and off, and they don't come any better than Lydia Fuentes. *She's* the one who wanted me to haul him in!''

Lisa looked at him with great scorn. ''So you're saying that you arrested Benny and stuck him in jail for two days as a favor to his grandmother?''

''Well...sort of.''

Lisa simply gazed at him, eyebrows raised in disbelief. Quinn could feel a flush rising in his cheeks. He went on hastily. ''This is a small town, Ms. Mendoza. We do things differently here.''

''I should say so if you arrest people and stick them in jail because their grandmother's mad at them!''

''That's not the way—''

''Look! I don't care what way you do things here! And don't try to con me with some lame story about his grandmother wanting you to arrest him. The fact is that you arrested Benny Hernandez without just cause, and you've been holding him without due process. If you persist in detaining him, I will obtain a writ of habeas corpus tomorrow to get him out, and then you and this county are going to be slapped with a big lawsuit for false imprisonment!''

Lisa stabbed the air with her forefinger as she talked, the force of her fury carrying her closer and closer to the sheriff until she was almost touching him with her punctuating finger. Quinn thought about wrapping his hand around her far smaller one and jerking her up against him, then silencing that berating voice with his own mouth.

That would be, he reminded himself, a good way

to get his face slapped. *Of course, it might be worth it....*

They stared into each other's face for a moment, poised on the edge. Lisa could see the red light burning in Quinn's brown eyes, feel the heat of his body only inches away from her, and something in her wanted to lean forward that last little bit, to precipitate some final explosion between them.

His jaw tightened, and he stepped carefully around her, going to the door and opening. "Padilla!" he barked. "Go down and release Hernandez. His attorney is taking him home."

Chapter 2

It was Deputy Padilla this time who escorted Lisa back to the locked double doors leading into the county jail. He spoke with the deputy inside, and a few minutes later, Jerry brought Benny Hernandez through the double doors, dressed this time in the usual jeans and T-shirt of a teenaged boy.

"Hey, you did it." He smiled, looking a little surprised.

"Can I give you a ride home?" Lisa didn't know whether the sheriff had literally meant that she would take him home. But in any case, she was a little curious to meet the young man's grandmother—*could the sheriff had been serious when he said the woman had asked him to lock up her grandson?*—and she couldn't imagine any place in this little town that would take her too far out of her way.

She drove through Angel Eye, following Benny's direction. The courthouse sat in the courthouse square typical of little Texas towns. A few stores lined the other sides of the street around it. It was not thriving, but neither did it look as abandoned as some little towns she had driven through. Past the stores, the streets were lined with trees, obviously planted and nurtured by the people who had lived there in the past, for outside of town, the landscape boasted little more than bushes of varying heights, yucca, and prickly pear cactus.

It was actually a rather pleasant-looking little town, Lisa thought, though she could not imagine what it must be like to grow up here. She had noticed when she drove into town that the population was just over sixteen hundred people, a mind-boggling concept to someone who had grown up in Dallas. The number of students attending her high school had been more than lived in this entire town. She had thought Hammond was small, but Angel Eye made it seem a positive metropolis.

She had never dreamed that she would wind up here. A scholarship she had applied for and received in law school had stipulated that she must spend the first year after she graduated doing legal aid work at one of the Hispanic organization's legal aid clinics. She had agreed readily to the terms, for she had already intended to use her law degree to help needy Hispanics. However, she had simply assumed that the work would be done in some large city, such as Houston or Dallas or San Antonio. It had never oc-

curred to her that the position she would fill would
be in Hammond, Texas, a town of little more than
ten thousand people about an hour's drive from San
Antonio. She had been certain she had landed in an
alien place when she drove down main street and saw
that the only two national fast-food chains in town
were lodged in the same building, sharing a kitchen
and eating space.

The first month she had lived in Hammond, she
had found herself making the six-hour drive back to
her parents' home in Dallas every weekend. Finally
that had grown too tiring, and now, after two months,
she was more or less resigned to remaining the rest
of her year there.

"What do people do around here?" she blurted
out, then realized a little guiltily that her words were
rather tactless.

Benny glanced at her, then chuckled. "Talk about
everybody else, mostly. Turn right at the next
street."

He straightened a little, and Lisa could see him
tense as they drove down the street. He pointed to a
small blue frame house, and Lisa pulled up to the
curb in front of it. The front door opened, and a short
Hispanic woman bustled out of the front door. Lisa
had been picturing Benny's grandmother as a tradi-
tional-looking *abuelita,* with graying hair in a bun
and wearing a cotton housedress, so she was a little
surprised to see that while his grandmother's thick
black hair was streaked with gray, it was cropped

short, and her rather squat body was encased in blue pants and a flowered top.

Benny groaned and cast a glance at Lisa. "You'll have to meet her. I'm sorry."

"I would like to meet your grandmother," Lisa assured him and stepped out of the car.

Señora Fuentes was crying and talking at great length in Spanish, and she did not pause in either activity when she threw her arms around her grandson and squeezed him to her. Finally she released him and stepped back, looking up at him.

"What are you doing home so quick?" she asked, planting her hands on her hips and gazing at him sternly. Lisa, listening, had the feeling that maybe Sheriff Sutton had been telling the truth, after all. Benny's grandmother, after her initial greeting, did not seem to be too pleased at having him home.

Benny, who had been grinning and looking faintly embarrassed a moment earlier, adopted his former blank expression. He shrugged. "He didn't have anything on me. He was messing with me."

"Messing with you?" the old woman repeated, contempt tinging her voice. "I think it's the other way, you messin' with the law." She launched forth into another spate of Spanish, this one by the look and sound of it, a stern lecture on Benny's troublesome ways.

Benny crossed his arms and gazed down at the ground as the old woman went on and on, and with every sentence, Lisa could see his jaw tighten. Finally, flinging his arms up, he shot back a short sentence in the same language and turned away, striding off down the sidewalk away from the house.

His grandmother looked after him for a moment, then swung around to face Lisa. She started to speak in Spanish again, and Lisa held up her hands to stop the rapid flow of words.

"*Señora,* no, please, *no comprendo. Yo no hablo español.*"

Señora Fuentes stopped, a puzzled frown settling on her face. "Oh. I'm sorry. I thought—you are not Latina?"

"Yes, I am," Lisa protested quickly, feeling the familiar embarrassment and faint sense of being different. "At least on my father's side. It's just—I'm afraid I don't speak Spanish." The old woman continued to look at her, as though trying to understand how this could be. Lisa hurried on, "My name is Lisa Mendoza, Señora Fuentes. I am your grandson Benny's attorney. I got him released from jail."

"You did?" Señora Fuentes looked her up and down. "But you are a girl."

Lisa struggled to suppress her irritation, reminding herself that this woman was old and unused to seeing women, especially Hispanic women, in positions of strength. Patiently, she said, "Yes, I am a woman. I am also an attorney."

Señora shook her head, disappointment stamping her face. "I never thought the sheriff would give in to a bit of a girl."

Lisa straightened, her eyes flashing. "Señora Fuentes, I am not 'a bit of a girl.' I am a grown woman and a lawyer, and Sheriff Sutton did not 'give in' to me. He had no reason to hold your grandson. He knew he could not continue to keep him in jail once an attorney was representing him. I would think you would be glad to know that Benny's cousin went to the trouble and expense of getting him an attorney instead of letting him rot in jail!''

"Cousin?" Señora Fuentes's brows drew together darkly. "He doesn't have any cousins old enough to—you don't mean Julio!''

"No. His name was Enrique Garza.''

"I don't know this man," Señora Fuentes said pugnaciously. "Who is this Garza? There is no cousin named Garza.''

"I beg your pardon?" Lisa looked at her blankly.

"Benny has no cousin named Enrique Garza.'' Señora Fuentes looked at her suspiciously.

Lisa simply gazed back at her, nonplussed. "But I—he came into my office and said he was Benny's cousin. He explained Benny's situation to me and said he wanted to help him.''

"He is one of them," Benny's grandmother said flatly, her lips drawing into a thin line.

"Who?''

"The bad men. The ones he goes to see. *Cholos. Vatos.*'' Her lips twisted bitterly, and tears sprang into her black eyes. "I will lose him. Like I lost Pablo.''

"Señora Fuentes…" Lisa reached out to touch the woman's arm, sympathy springing up in her at the woman's evident sorrow. "Can I help you?''

But the other woman twisted away. "No." She cast Lisa a dark glance. "Go away from here. You have done enough."

She turned and walked back into the house. Lisa watched her go, feeling vaguely guilty. Finally, with a sigh, she turned and went back to her car. She got in and turned the car around, driving back the way she had come. There was no reason for her to feel guilty, she told herself. She had gotten her client out of jail; she had protected his rights. The sheriff had had no business taking him in in the first place.

But logic had a hard time standing up against the look of suffering in the old woman's eyes. Lisa kept thinking about it, wishing that she could have made Benny's grandmother understand that she had helped Benny.

A few blocks down the street, she saw Benny walking along, hands jammed in his pockets, head down. She pulled her car to a stop beside him and pushed the button to roll down the window. "Benny? Do you need a ride?"

He looked over at her and started to shake his head, but in the next instant, he stopped, then said, "Hey, yeah." He walked over to the car and leaned down, looking into the window. "You could drop me off at the café, if you don't mind."

"No, it's okay. Where is it?"

It didn't take long to reach the café. It was on the same main street of Angel Eye that they had driven along when they'd left the courthouse, but farther out, almost on the edge of town. It was a small, plain building set back from the road, with a modest sign at the front of the parking lot proclaiming it to be Moonstone Café.

"Moonstone Café? That's an odd name." Lisa said as she turned into the parking lot. She had thought that an eating place in this little town would be named something like Earl's Diner or Martha's.

"Yeah. Lady owns it is from Dallas," Benny said, as if that fact would explain all peculiarity. "It's good. You should try it."

"Maybe I will."

"Well…thanks." Benny got out of the car and gave her an awkward wave, then walked into the restaurant.

Lisa watched him go. It occurred to her that she was hungry. And it *was* the end of the day; everyone would have left the office by the time she got there. Perhaps she should give this oddly named restaurant a try. The mere fact that its owner was from Dallas gave it some appeal to her.

She parked her car and followed her client through the front door of the restaurant. A slim woman with thick curling dark hair turned from the cash register and smiled at her.

"One for dinner?" she asked. Lisa nodded, and the woman led her toward a booth in front of one of the windows.

Lisa glanced around the restaurant as she followed the woman. It was a neat, clean place, nothing fancy, just wooden tables and comfortable chairs and booths, but it was obviously popular. Even as early as it was, several of the tables were occupied. There was a smell of fresh-baked bread in the air, mingling enticingly with garlic and spices.

She noticed that her client was standing near the kitchen door, talking with a pretty, slender Hispanic girl. Benny's face was more animated than it had been the entire time she had been around him, and the way he stood before the girl, bending down toward her in a tender, even protective way, spoke volumes about what he felt for her. And, given the glow on the young girl's face as she looked back at him, it appeared that she returned the feeling.

The woman who had seated her followed her gaze, and she smiled. "Ah, young love." She handed a menu to Lisa. "Don't worry. Teresa will be over here in a minute. She's a good waitress. You new around here?"

"I live in Hammond," Lisa replied. "But I'm new there. I'm from Dallas."

"Yeah?" The other woman smiled. "Me, too. I'm Elizabeth Morgan. I own the Moonstone."

"Lisa Mendoza. Nice to meet you. So you moved here from Dallas?"

Elizabeth Morgan laughed at the tone of amazement that crept into Lisa's voice as she asked the question. "I wanted to get far away from Dallas."

"Well, you certainly achieved that."

"Yeah. It's pretty different. But I like a little town. It's…cozy, I guess. I was starting over, and it wasn't as expensive to start a restaurant in a small town."

"Don't you miss Dallas?"

"Sometimes." Elizabeth shrugged. "I mean, it's nice to have a big choice of movies to go see, malls to go shopping at, other restaurants to eat in. But you know, frankly, when you run a restaurant, you're tied to it. Twenty-four seven. You don't get out that much to do any of those things, and if I want to, well, San Antonio's not that far away. The rest of the time, there's the fact that it takes me five minutes to get to work; there's very little turnover in employees; and I know most of my customers by name. I like that."

They were interrupted at that point by the arrival of the young girl who had been talking to Benny earlier. "I'm sorry," she said a little breathlessly. "Sorry, Ms. Morgan."

Elizabeth smiled and nodded to Lisa. "I'll get back to my job and let you order now. It was nice chatting with you."

She moved away, and the girl went into her spiel. "My name is Teresa, and I'll be waiting on you this evening. Could I get you a drink while you look over the menu?"

Lisa ordered and settled back into the booth to relax. Benny, she noticed, had disappeared. She found her thoughts turning to Sheriff Sutton. *The man was damnably attractive.* She remembered that moment in his office when they had been only inches apart, white-hot anger coursing through her, and mingled with it, feeding off it, had been a pulsing, primitive desire. She had felt it coming off him, too, humming and magnetic.

It was absurd, of course, Lisa reminded herself. They were, literally, on opposites sides. And she felt certain that they had nothing in common, no real attraction except for that strange, momentary response. A chemical reaction, that's all. Some animal impulse, spurred by a signal too primal for her to even notice—a scent or a visual stimulus—the line of his leg against his uniform, perhaps, or his long, mobile fingers, thumb hooked into the belt of his uniform, or the well-cut lips…

Lisa realized with a start that she was sitting staring at the table dreamily, a faint smile curving her mouth. She had started out analyzing her bizarre response to the man, and she had wound up daydreaming about him like a teenager in class!

She was glad when Teresa brought her salad, giving her something to concentrate on besides the sheriff. The meal, she discovered to her delight, was delicious—the salad crisp and dark green, the barest of balsamic vinaigrette on it, just as she liked it, and the pasta dish light and subtly seasoned.

"How was your dinner?" Elizabeth Morgan stopped by her table on the way back from seating some more customers.

"Wonderful," Lisa replied truthfully. "As good as in Dallas."

Elizabeth smiled at the phrasing of her praise. "I take it that you miss Dallas?"

"Yeah." Lisa let out a regretful sigh. "Although, I have to admit, not as much after a dinner like this one."

Elizabeth lingered by her table for a few minutes, chatting with her about Dallas, and Teresa came to clear the dishes from her table and bring her bill. She had just paid her bill when the door of the café opened and Sheriff Sutton strode in.

He glanced around, then walked purposefully toward Lisa's table. *What was it,* Lisa wondered, *that was so utterly sexy about the way a man walked in cowboy boots?*

Beside her, echoing her thoughts, Elizabeth Morgan let out an exaggerated sigh and said, "Sheriffs have got it all over cops, don't they? There's just something about boots and a cowboy hat." She smiled at Sutton as he drew near. "Good evening, Sheriff. You want to see a menu?"

"No, thanks, Elizabeth. I'm not staying. I just wanted to talk to Ms. Mendoza."

"Sure. You want something to drink? Coffee? Iced tea?"

"Coffee would be great, thanks."

Elizabeth moved away as he slid into the booth across from Lisa.

"Have a seat," Lisa commented dryly.

He grinned. "Thanks."

"What are you doing here?"

"I saw your car outside. Thought I'd drop by and talk to you a little bit."

"How do you know my car?" She asked, exasperated.

"Saw you get into it a while ago." Again the

bone-melting smile flashed as he admitted, "I was watching out my window when you left."

"Sheriff...I don't know what you want, but—"

"You know, I just got my butt chewed out for about ten minutes by Benny's grandmother for letting you get Benny away from me. You owe me a few minutes of your time."

Lisa could not help but smile at the image of that short old woman raking Quinn Sutton over the coals. "Sorry. I've met the wrath of Señora Fuentes myself."

"Look, Ms. Mendoza..." Quinn leaned across the table, looking into Lisa's eyes. Lisa found it difficult to look away. "I think we got off on the wrong foot. I was thinking that maybe we could start all over again. If you knew me better, you might find out that I'm not such an ogre."

"I am sure you are not," Lisa agreed easily. "However, I see little use in getting to know you, as you say. We are on opposite sides, and—"

"We're not so far apart as you think," he put in quickly. "I realize that you don't think so, but I have Benny Hernandez's best interests at heart."

Lisa leaned back against the padded seat of the booth, crossing her arms and raising her eyebrows expressively. "You do?"

"Yes, I do. I don't know what you're used to. Obviously you come from the city somewhere. San Antonio? Houston?"

"Dallas."

He nodded. "Well, things are different here. I

don't look on the sheriff's job as getting criminals so much as protecting the people of the town. People like Señora Fuentes, for instance. And her grandson, little as you would like to believe it. I am trying to help Benny.''

''I see. So you are sort of the Great White Father of Angel Eye, is that it? Protecting all the poor and ignorant Mexicans, even if it means incarcerating them illegally.''

Sutton's jaw tightened. ''You know, you've got a hell of a chip on your shoulder—especially considering the fact that I can speak Spanish better than you can.''

Fury spurted up in Lisa at his words. She grabbed her purse and scooted out of the booth, sending a flashing angry glance at him before striding quickly out of the restaurant.

As she strode across the parking lot, she heard his bootsteps on the pavement behind her, but she ignored him, marching straight to her car. He caught up with her before she reached it, grasping her arm and pulling her to a halt.

Lisa spun around, jerking her arm from his grasp. Her skin seemed to burn where he had touched it, and her anger was fueled by the fact that his nearness, his touch, made her feel weak in the knees. ''Let go of me! What do you think you're doing?''

''I'm sorry. Don't go storming off. I'm trying to explain things to you. I'm trying to make amends.''

''You're doing a really lousy job of it.''

''I know,'' he agreed ruefully. ''I seem to have a

knack for offending you. Please, ignore what I said. You're off base in saying that I'm acting out of prejudice, but I understand why you'd feel that way. This isn't about singling Benny Hernandez out because he's a Latino. Maybe I'm too paternal in the way I feel about this town, but it isn't only regarding the Mexican-American community. I have a duty to help the people of this town, to protect them. That's what I was elected to do. That's why I haul the kids I catch drinking and driving down to the jail, not because I enjoy hassling drunk teenagers or causing their parents grief, but because I want them to think before they do it next time. I don't want to have to scrape them up off the road.''

"No doubt that's admirable. But we are not talking about a drunken teenager here. We're talking about a trumped-up charge, and I don't care if Benny's grandmother wanted you to teach him a lesson or whatever, you violated that young man's rights.''

"It isn't always that black and white," he responded tightly. Quinn truthfully had come to apologize and make things right with Lisa. He had been thinking about her ever since she'd left the courthouse this afternoon, and when he had spotted her car in the parking lot of the Moonstone, it had seemed a heaven-sent opportunity to make a fresh start with her. But somehow, as before, he had wound up right back in an argument with her. And, as before, his loins tightened involuntarily at the sight of her, cheeks flushed, eyes bright with fury, her curvaceous body thrumming with tension.

What was it about this woman that made him respond at the basest level? She filled him with the hot lust to subdue her, to kiss her until she melted beneath him, her fury transforming into passion beneath his touch. He balled his hands into fists and tried to shove down the distinctly erotic images that were flooding his mind.

''Will you let me explain to you?'' he asked, keeping his voice carefully neutral.

''Please do.'' Lisa crossed her arms over her chest and waited, her gaze challenging.

''Look. I'm going to be straight with you. Benny's grandmother came to me because she was worried about him. He's gotten into a few scrapes with the law over the years, but he's not a bad kid. But because of his father and stepfather and her own son Pablo, she's worried about him. She called me and told me that he's hanging out with a bad bunch of guys. He used to work over here at the Moonstone, busing tables, but then he quit and now he doesn't have any job. But he never asks her for money, not for clothes or gas or burgers or anything. Where is he getting his money? And he's gone a lot. She tells me that she thinks his friends are a bad influence, especially this kid named Paco.

''Now, it so happens that this Paco is frequently seen at a house in town where suspicious things are going on. When she told me Benny was hanging with Paco it worried me, too. I've been keeping a close eye on this house and you know what? Now I've seen Benny over there, too.''

"That's it?" Lisa asked. "You've seen him at some other house? Where suspicious things are going on? What suspicious things? And he has a friend that his grandmother doesn't like?"

"I can't tell you what's going on at this house. I'm not even sure yet myself. But I can pretty much guarantee you that it isn't legal. There are a lot of kids coming and going at this house, and only some of them are from Angel Eye. That outside element adds something serious to it."

"This sounds extremely vague. You have no evidence of a crime."

"Not yet. But I will have. And I would hate for Benny to have been sucked into it. In this part of the country, especially with those outside people involved, the odds are it's large-scale auto theft, drugs or smuggling illegal aliens. Those aren't minor offenses. I'd like to get Benny out of if before it's too late."

"Oh, I see. So you hauled him down to jail and questioned him for hours without an attorney present just because you were concerned about him. It didn't have anything to do with trying to get information out of him about this house and these activities that you know so little about?"

"Why are you so all-fired determined to dislike me?" he shot back. "I'm telling you things I wouldn't normally reveal to a suspect's attorney. To anyone, in fact. I'm giving you information about an ongoing investigation, because I want to help Benny, not put him in prison. I am trying to make you understand why it's so important.''

"Why?" Lisa asked bluntly.

"What? What do you mean?"

"Why are you telling me this? Are you hoping that I will encourage my client to tell you what you want to know? Is that it?''

Quinn clenched his teeth together, a muscle in his jaw jumping. "You are the most exasperating, pigheaded woman I ever had the misfortune to meet." It did not help his irritation any that he knew he was laying out his reasons for her partly because he hated for her to continue thinking of him as a bumbling redneck going around trampling on the rights of others.

"Why, thank you," Lisa told him sweetly. "You have certainly succeeded in winning me over now."

She turned on her heel and started toward her car again.

"Wait!" He hurried after her and stepped in front of her, facing her, forcing her to stop. "Think about this—who is Enrique Garza? He's no cousin to Benny Hernandez."

"So? He's a friend, I suppose."

"Deputy Padilla says he's not from Angel Eye. I don't think he's any friend to Benny. Why don't you ask yourself why he is so eager to help some kid who's been picked up on petty charges? What's in it for him? I'm sure he didn't do it out of the goodness of his heart."

"Who he is does not change my job. I am Benny Hernandez's attorney, and my duty is to protect his rights."

"Well, I'm sure you'll get a chance to do that when he's hauled in on auto theft or marijuana-smuggling. You know, you might think about *helping* your client, not just representing him in court."

He whirled and took a few steps away from her, then stopped, muttering a curse beneath his breath. He turned and covered the distance between them in two quick strides. Grabbing Lisa by the arms, he pulled her up against him and buried his lips in hers.

Chapter 3

At the touch of Quinn's lips on hers, desire burst through Lisa. The intensity and ferocity of her hunger was overwhelming. Every atom in her body seemed suddenly alive and pulsing, every nerve throbbing with sensation. His lips were smooth and hot, pressing into hers, opening her mouth to him. His hands left their grip on her arms, one of them sliding behind her back, pulling her even more tightly into his hard body. His other hand came up to the back of her head, tangling in her hair, fingertips pressing into her scalp.

Without thinking, she slid her arms around his neck, pressing herself up into him as her lips responded hungrily to his. She trembled, clinging to Quinn, as lust unfurled deep inside her abdomen, hot and aching. Her breasts were pressed against the hard bones of his chest; she could feel the line of his body all up and down her own.

Then, abruptly, his arms loosened around her, and he raised his head. He looked down into her face, his eyes lit with a red fire. The heat of his body surrounded her; his arm was like iron against her back. Lisa sagged against it, too numb to speak or even think. Her mouth was slightly open in bemusement, her lips soft and faintly moist, darkened from the bruising pressure of his kiss. Quinn sucked in his breath, hunger slamming through him with the force of a freight train.

But he was also aware of the windows of the restaurant behind him and the wide sweep of street in front of him, and he knew that if he continued, the gossip would be all over town tomorrow.

He tried to speak and it came out a croak. He cleared his throat, his arms sliding away from Lisa, and tried to bring his scrambled brains back into sufficient order to make sense.

"Oh, God!" Lisa squeaked, her hand clapping over her mouth, her brown eyes huge and horrified above her hand. "Oh, no!"

She whirled and almost ran to her car. Quinn stood and watched her go, having no words to stop her. The engine of her car roared to life and she whipped out of the parking space, then tore out into the street in a squeal of tires. Quinn pulled in a deep breath.

What in the hell had just happened?

He remained standing there for a long moment before he got into his car and drove home in a state of profound disquiet.

Sitting in front of the small, old-fashioned brick house where he lived was an ice-blue BMW, which could belong to only one person he knew.

"Hey, Cater," he said as he swung out of the patrol car and cut across the lawn toward his front steps.

"Hey, bro," the black-haired man sitting on the top step replied, standing up. "How you doing?"

"Not too well at the moment. What are you doing here?"

The other man's brows rose and he replied in a mocking way, "Well, I'm doing fine. Thank you very much for asking. I always appreciate it when my brother is so pleased to see me."

"Sorry." Quinn took the front steps two at a time and stopped beside his brother.

Cater, almost exactly the same height as his younger brother, was dark-haired like most of the rest of the family, and his eyes, under straight black brows, were a deep blue. Generally considered the most handsome of the Sutton brothers, there was about him an air of sophistication that usually earned him a good deal of ribbing from Quinn and their older brother Daniel. A successful author of mystery novels, he lived in Austin, but he had bought a piece of land near Angel Eye and built a small house on it, which he frequently visited.

"Bad day?" Cater asked.

Quinn shrugged. "An unusual one. I haven't yet
decided whether it's bad or good. Come on in." He
unlocked the door and opened it, leading the way
inside and calling back over his shoulder, "You want
a beer? I could sure use one."

"Sure." Cater trailed after him.

A cat jumped down from the windowsill and
stalked toward Quinn, meowing plaintively. The cat
was big, and few would call him attractive. Orange
in color, his tail was unnaturally short, and the tip of
one ear had a small chunk missing. A scar curved
down over one eye and across his nose, and another
short, thick scar cut through the fur on the top of its
head. He looked like what he was, an old fighter, and
he had adopted Quinn a couple of years earlier. Apparently Quinn was as far as his affection for humans
would go, for he treated everyone else with contempt. He cast a dismissive glance toward Cater now,
then twined himself around Quinn's legs, complain-
ing at length until Quinn dished out some food for
him.

Cater sat down at the old wooden table in the
kitchen, watching Quinn. It amused him a little that
Quinn, the hard-bitten cop, was the sentimentalist of
the family and had been the one horrified when their
father intended to give away the old wooden kitchen
table that had sat in their grandparents' kitchen since
the 1920s. He had taken it back with him to his apartment in San Antonio and since then had been adding
furniture that complemented it, until now his small
house was almost entirely furnished with Texas

farmhouse antiques. The furniture suited the little house, too. It had been built in the 1920s, with the sharply peaked gables of the era that always brought to Cater's mind the witches' houses of his childhood fairy tales. The house had been run-down, and Quinn maintained that he had bought it because it was such a bargain, but anyone who had seen the amount of time and sweat he had poured into restoring and repairing the building knew that it had been much more a labor of love and art than a business decision.

"You come down early for Daniel's wedding?" Quinn asked, setting down two bottles of beer on the table and swinging one of the chairs around to straddle it as he faced his brother, crossing his arms on the back of the chair.

"Yeah. I sent off my proposal for my next book, and I figured I would take a few days' rest. A week after the wedding I have to go on tour, so I thought a reward in advance was in order."

"Your new book's out?"

"Next week." He grimaced. "It'd be great if it weren't for two weeks of living in hotels and flying so many places I hardly know where I am."

"Shall I get out the violin?" Quinn joked.

"I know. I know. I'm an ungrateful jerk. I should be glad people want to meet me and buy my book. And I am. I just hate all those airports."

"I wouldn't know about that, being a country boy myself." Quinn took a swig from the bottle. "Where's Cory? Did he come down with you?"

Cory was another brother, the youngest child in

the family, now in his senior year at the University of Texas at Austin. He lived in a garage apartment behind Cater's turn-of-the-century house.

"Nah. He's coming down Friday. He's doing his student teaching this semester, thinks the school would crumble if he missed a day or two."

Quinn shook his head. "Who'd a thought that boy would decide to be a schoolteacher? After all the trouble he used to cause."

Cater snorted. "Look who's talking. You are, if I remember correctly, the one who set fires in the trashcans behind the high school."

"Now, that was all a mistake," Quinn protested.

"Sheriff didn't seem to think so."

Quinn groaned. "I thought Dad was going to bust a blood vessel that time."

"It was your getting in trouble with Sheriff Woods," Cater said. "He didn't want to have to be beholden to the man."

"Yeah, I know. Woods was a dangerous guy, whether he was a friend or an enemy."

"What do you know about him?" Cater asked casually.

"Not much. Mostly what everybody else knew, I guess. You didn't cross the man, not in this county. Other than that…well, he was a political power, the kind that swung elections, even if he had to vote all the residents of the cemetery to do it. It would be my guess that there were a few skeletons in his closet."

"You know anything about his death?"

Quinn shook his head. "No. Nothing but the facts of it. I was in college when it happened. Long time, probably ten years, before I came back here. Why?"

"I'm looking into it a little. I've been thinking about writing a book about it."

"Oh, great!" Quinn groaned. "As if I didn't have enough problems.... First I got some crime ring operating here, only I can't figure out what the hell is going on or who's behind it—all I know is that a suspicious number of young men are going in and out of old man Rodriquez's house at all hours, some of them complete strangers to this town. Lots of different cars parked there, some of them nice. Then I have to be insanely attracted to this defense attorney who's threatened to sue me, and now my own brother is going to stir up some ancient scandal in the sheriff's office!"

"Don't worry about it. I'm not even certain about doing it yet. I have another book to write first. I'm only toying with the idea. Murdered sheriff... scandal...pretty intriguing stuff. But it'll be fiction. I've never written true crime. I'll use it as a starting place."

"That's faint comfort," Quinn retorted. "Everybody will know it was a true story, so they'll believe whatever you write is true, even the stuff you make up." He pointed his index finger at his brother warningly. "Just don't involve the guy who becomes sheriff a decade later." He paused, then added with a grin, "'Course, I guess if you wanted to make him the hero who solves everything, you could."

Cater's snort promised little hope of that happening. "Yeah, right. But what I want to know is— what's this about a defense lawyer? Male or female?"

"Female, you idiot. Her name's Lisa Mendoza, and she's about as pretty as they come. And she thinks I'm a redneck good ol' boy who's harassing her client and miscarrying justice whenever I get the opportunity."

"I see. Doesn't sound too hopeful."

Quinn grinned in his familiar cocky way. "Don't worry. I'll bring her around."

Cater couldn't resist smiling at his brother's attitude, but he shook his head. "One day, brother, you are going to take a hard fall at the hands of some woman, and then you'll find out what it's like."

Quinn offered him a faint smile, saying, "Who knows? Maybe I already have."

Lisa blasted down the farm-to-market road toward Hammond, scarcely noticing anything she passed. Afterward, she was grateful for the rural lack of traffic on the road, as well as the absence of police. Her mind was not on her driving.

She had never experienced a kiss like that before. It was like something out of a book, a movie. She had enjoyed the kisses she had shared with other men, had felt passion and desire. But this! This was different. Never before had she felt as if every nerve in her body was standing on end, or as if she burned from the inside out. When Quinn had kissed her, she had melted. Electricity had shot through her. Every romantic cliché she could think of had happened to her—only it had not been clichéd at all, but real and thrilling.

It was crazy, she thought. Wonderful, too, but definitely crazy. She did not even like the man. He was arrogant, cocky, and bullheaded. He obviously didn't care about following the dictates of the law, only about getting what he wanted, and it was clear from that grin that he was used to getting what he wanted from women, as well. He was precisely the sort of man whom she most disliked.

So how could a kiss from that man have affected her like that? How could he have made her feel as if she were about to fall into an old-fashioned swoon?

Lisa had always been someone in control of herself and her life. Even her teenage years had contained only a minimum number of tantrums and crushes. Mostly she had maintained an even keel: dating, studying, working—keeping everything in proportion. She was an intelligent girl, accustomed to being ruled by her head, and she had always hated the classic stereotype of the tempestuous, passionate Latina.

Somehow Quinn Sutton had shattered all that with one kiss.

She turned into the parking lot of her apartment, faintly surprised to find that she had already made it home. She parked and turned off the engine, then sat for a moment, her hands still gripping the steering wheel. Her head dropped to her hands.

It was vital that she get a grip on this, she told herself. She was not about to start letting her passions rule her life at this late date. *What had really happened this afternoon, anyway?* It was not as if she had fallen in love with the man or fallen into bed with him, she pointed out reasonably. They had shared a kiss, that was all, and Quinn Sutton had proved to be a superior kisser to anyone she had ever met. *That was all.*

It was what she made of it that was important, and the worst thing would be to attach a significance to the moment that it did not have. The thing for her to do, she knew, was to get on with her life. The things that were important to her were her work and her family; Quinn Sutton did not matter to either of those things, except as a possible adversary. The odds were that she would not even see him again.

Firmly she ignored the deflation that went through her at that thought. The thing to do, she decided, was to put the kiss out of her mind, to reject it as the aberration that it was. With that resolve, she got out of her car, locked it, and went inside her apartment, doing her best to ignore the weakness that remained in her legs.

An evening of cleaning up her apartment helped to quell thoughts of her encounter with the sheriff— although she found herself all too often simply standing and staring sightlessly at the wall, work forgotten, and she had to shake herself and return to the job at hand. The evening crept by, and it was something of a relief when it grew late enough for her to go to bed. But she found once she lay down that sleep would not come. Instead, her mind returned to her encounter with Quinn Sutton. She went over their arguments, coming up with clever retorts that she had not had the presence of mind to think of at the time and remembering, too, the tilt of his head, the way his shoulders filled out his uniform, his walk as he strode across the restaurant toward her. The eyes of every woman in the place had been on him, she was sure of that.

Most of all, she relived that moment in the parking lot when he had kissed her, feeling all over again— though never, disappointingly, with quite the same intensity—the sensations that had flooded her when his lips touched hers. No matter how she tried, she could not banish the thought from her mind, and as a result, half the night had gone by before she at last fell asleep.

The next morning she awoke heavy-lidded and tired, but she pushed through the day determinedly. She drove to her office in a plain brick building a few blocks from the center of Hammond. It was there that the Texas Hispanic League maintained its legal aid office. Her office was a small one tucked into one corner of the second floor. It was provided by the League and she shared the services of a secretary with one of the other lawyers. She was required to handle a certain proportion of the work of the legal aid office, but it was not really enough to fill her time, and the stipend she received from them was barely enough to get by, so she was also free to take on other legal work that might come in. Most of that extra work, like Benny's case, was in the area of criminal law, and it generally involved acting as a court-appointed attorney, paid for by the state. A customer who paid out of his pocket, like Mr. Garza had done for Benny, was something of a rarity.

Her thoughts, having gone to Enrique Garza, stayed there. Given the reaction of Benny's grandmother when she had told her who had hired her to represent Benny, she was inclined to think that Sutton was right: Benny was involved in something, and Garza was involved in it as well. He obviously was not a relative or friend; Señora Fuentes would have recognized his name if he had been. The odds were he was not even someone from Angel Eye, a town small enough that surely Benny's grandmother or someone in the sheriff's office would have heard of him. Just as obviously, Benny had recognized the name, for his look of puzzlement had changed immediately to a carefully blank expression. And there was little reason to suppose that someone who was not a relative or friend would have gone to the trouble and expense of hiring an attorney to get Benny out of jail. But if Benny were involved in something illegal and Garza was involved in it, too, he very well might pay in order to make sure that Benny didn't tell the sheriff all about it.

She frowned, remembering the contempt in the sheriff's voice as he had told her that she ought to help her client rather than merely represent him in court. That was what she would do, she argued mentally. She would help Benny, but the scope of her help was professional, after all, devoted only to legal problems. It did not include seeing that her client stuck to the straight and narrow or stayed away from bad influences. To expect a lawyer to do that would be like expecting one's doctor to hang around supervising one's diet or exercise program or reminding them to take their pills. She was there to represent Benny, that was all. And the fact that Mr. Garza might have pretended to be someone he was not did not change her duty to her client.

Lisa stood up and walked out to the small open area where her secretary sat at a desk, busily typing on a word processor. "Kiki…?"

The secretary turned toward her inquiringly, her fingers pausing on the keys. "Yes?"

"You know that man who came in here yesterday afternoon…Mr. Garza? Had you ever seen him before? Did you recognize him?"

"No." Kiki frowned thoughtfully. "I didn't know him. I just remember thinking that he was dressed awfully nice to be coming here."

Lisa thought back, trying to remember what the man had had on. It had been a suit, fashionable and rather expensive looking, as she recalled. Kiki was right; their clients were generally far too poor to be able to afford a suit like that.

"My guess is he wasn't from around here," Kiki went on. "Nobody in Hammond dresses like that."

"True." Hammond, like Angel Eye, ran more to jeans and boots and work shirts, and when a man wore a suit here it was definitely not as stylish or as well-made as that Enrique Garza had worn yesterday. "He looked like he was from the city, didn't he?"

Kiki nodded in agreement. "Why? Who is this guy? What did he want?"

"He wanted me to get someone out of jail. And the kid shouldn't have been in there. But Mr. Garza told me he was the kid's cousin and he isn't. Just wondering why he's lying to me."

"Sounds fishy."

"Yeah." Lisa turned away, hesitated, then turned back. "Do you, ah, do you know Sheriff Sutton?"

"Quinn?" The other woman's face smiled, her eyes warming. "Sure. Everybody knows Quinn Sutton. Is that the jail your client was in?"

Lisa nodded.

"Did you meet Quinn?" Kiki continued enthusiastically. "Isn't he gorgeous? Well, I mean, maybe not gorgeous exactly. But there's something about him."

"His smile?" Lisa suggested a little sourly.

"Oh, yeah, definitely that. And there's that little twinkle in his eye, like he knows all kinds of wicked things…." Kiki sighed a little ruefully.

"I take it he's a ladies' man," Lisa added with great casualness.

"Yeah. He's dated lots of women. He's a terrible flirt. But charm!—that man's got it coming out of every pore."

"I suppose. I found him rather rude, personally."

"Quinn?" Her secretary look surprised. "I don't think I've ever seen him be rude. I heard he's got a bad temper, though. People say not to tangle with him."

"Well, he seems to be accustomed to bending the law to suit himself."

Kiki looked at her blankly. Obviously little had ever entered her head about the sheriff except his charm and looks. Lisa was not surprised by her secretary's description of Quinn Sutton. It had been clear that he was a flirt. She had no doubt that he had had lots of brief encounters with women, but no relationships. It was simply another reason to steer clear of him.

She went back into her office and tried once more to settle down to work. She was drawing up a will for a young single mother with little money but a need to establish guardianship for her children if she should die. Then there was a plea to draw up in a tort case that had grown out of a landlord/tenant dispute. It was one of the more interesting cases she had had since she'd moved to Hammond, and it held her interest enough that she was able to settle down to work and forget about Quinn Sutton for a while.

She spent the latter part of the afternoon looking up precedents in the office's small legal library down the hall, and she was a little surprised when she heard someone call her name and glanced up to see that it was after six o'clock. No doubt Kiki and most of the others had already left.

"Hello?" came the man's voice again. "Ms. Mendoza?"

"Yes?" she called, starting down the hallway toward the small area where the secretaries sat and which passed for a reception area as well.

A tall man in a sheriff's uniform was standing with his back toward her, looking toward the stairs. He held a light felt cowboy hat in his hands, which he slapped lightly against his leg as he waited. Lisa recognized the long, lean figure instantly, and her heart picked up its beat. She remembered their kiss of the evening before, and a thrill ran through her. She had to pause for an instant to school her features into calm.

"Sheriff Sutton?"

He turned around, a smile lightening his features, and Lisa could not help but smile back.

"Ms. Mendoza. Say, do you think, all things considered, we could drop the Sheriff and Ms. thing? I'm Quinn."

"My name is Lisa."

"Lisa." He nodded to her.

"Quinn."

"I had an errand to run over at the district courthouse," he went on. "So I thought I'd stop by. See if maybe I could persuade you to go out to supper with me."

Lisa was taken aback by how badly she wanted to accept. "Sheriff—I mean, Quinn—I, well, I don't think that would be appropriate."

He grinned. "I won't take you anyplace real rowdy. I promise."

"That's not what I meant, and you know it. We are on opposite sides. How would it look? I don't think it would be ethical for a defense attorney and the head of the county law enforcement to—"

"What? Have dinner together? I don't think it would turn all that many heads. You know, things are different in a small town."

"So you've told me. But ethics don't vary from city to rural areas."

"Look. In a little town, people know each other. You can't help it. And when you're involved in the same general thing, say, law, then you run into each other even more. It's not criminal to be friends with someone who's sometimes on the other side."

"We aren't exactly friends."

"Ah, but we could be." There was caressing note in his voice that promised something, but Lisa doubted that it was friendship. Being with a friend didn't make her nerves sizzle like being around this man did.

"Hell," he went on persuasively, "even in the city, I've seen D.A.s and defense attorneys grabbing lunch together. It's worse in a small town. You see each other in the courthouse, on the street, in restaurants. You can't avoid it. You just put aside the cases for the moment. Talk about something besides work."

"I don't think we have anything besides work to

talk about,'' Lisa said pointedly. ''And I have a lot
of work to do. I really can't spare the time.''

''To eat?'' He made a comical face of amazement.

''You know,'' she remarked with some asperity,
''persistence is not necessarily a virtue.''

''Well, I wasn't really trying to be virtuous.''

Lisa could not keep from letting out a chuckle, and
Quinn quickly pursued his advantage, ''What about
drinks, then? That wouldn't take long. We'll run
down to the steakhouse. It has a bar, and we can get
a quick drink. Then you can come back to work if
you have to.''

Lisa hesitated. She could not keep that kiss last
night out of her mind. Perhaps if she spent a little
time with him, she would be reminded of all the reasons why she didn't like the man, and the memory
of the kiss would fade. Another voice inside warned
that she might find out just the opposite, but she ignored it. ''All right,'' she agreed finally, adding
warningly, ''But just drinks.''

Quinn grinned, knowing he'd won. ''Whatever
you say, ma'am.''

He offered her his arm, and Lisa took it. The
quiver that ran through her at even this touch told
her that she had probably just made a huge mistake.
But she could not summon up a bit of regret as they
started down the stairs. She was too filled with a
bubbling sense of anticipation.

Chapter 4

The steakhouse to which Quinn took her was an old-fashioned place, with brick interior walls and red leather booths and chairs, lit dimly, candles in squat red holders on all the tables lending a warm glow. They sat at a small intimate table in the bar, and Quinn asked her what drink she would like.

"Oh, a gin and tonic, I think." She glanced at him, a smile teasing at her lips. "Let me guess—you're going to get a beer—no, wait, a bourbon."

He chuckled. "You got me there." When the waitress came, he ordered a bourbon.

"You think you've got me all figured out, don't you?" he asked her, smiling. "Good old boy, redneck sheriff."

"Ladies' man."

He managed a wounded look. "Now where'd you hear that?"

"I didn't have to hear it. I figured that out all on my own."

"You ought to know better than that," he said teasingly. "People are more complicated than they seem on first impression. Take you, for example."

"Me?"

"Yeah. You've got a few contradictions."

"Oh." Lisa grimaced. "You mean my not being able to speak Spanish."

"That and some other things. The way you talk, your mannerisms—now don't bite my head off, but you don't seem like any of the Latina girls I grew up with."

"Maybe that's more your prejudices showing than my contradictions."

"Tell me this, did you have your *quinteñera?*" he asked, mentioning the debutlike celebration common among Hispanic girls when they reached the age of fifteen.

Lisa frowned at him and grudgingly admitted, "No, I did not. And we never made tamales at Christmas, either. Or even celebrated Cinco de Mayo. But that doesn't mean that I'm not Hispanic."

"I never said you weren't. I'm just saying that people are more complicated than their stereotypes."

"All right. Point taken." Lisa sighed. "My father is Latino. My mother's Anglo. But I grew up all Anglo. Even Daddy can't speak Spanish—I mean, he knows some phrases and stuff, but he couldn't carry on a conversation in it. His parents were the cook and gardener for this wealthy family in Amarillo, and they lived in the servants' quarters behind the house, so they lived in a very Anglo, rich community, and he went to a neighborhood school, where all the kids were Anglo. He didn't even have big family get-togethers. His parents had left all their relatives behind in Mexico. Their goal in life was for him to be successful. They wanted him to get a good education, go to college, make money. It was what they came to the U.S. for.''

''Nothing wrong with that. Sounds like the typical immigrants' dream. That's what everybody's ancestors came here for.''

''All they wanted was good for him,'' Lisa agreed. ''But, I don't know, it seems that they rejected his heritage to do it. They didn't let him speak Spanish even in their home. They didn't want him to have an accent, they wanted him to be like all the other kids. That's what he wanted, too—to be like everyone else, to be a success. He was smart and he got scholarships, and he went to college then dental school. Even though it was the sixties, he never got into the whole Chicano movement. He wasn't political; he just wanted to make good grades and go on to make good money. Then he married my mom, and she's Anglo, and they settled down in Dallas and—well, I had a very upper-middle-class, Anglo upbringing.''

Quinn shrugged. ''That's not a crime.''

''No. But sometimes it makes me feel...embarrassed. Like I was a traitor to my people. Except for

my name and having black hair and skin that tans easily, there was nothing Hispanic about my life. I mean,
we didn't even go to the Catholic Church. All my
friends were Anglo. I never felt like I was any different
from them. Robby Maldenado was the only other Mexican-American in our whole circle of friends, and he
was just like me.''

''So what happened?''

''What do you mean?''

''Well, here you are in Hammond, working for the
Texas Hispanic League legal aid office, rescuing
Mexican-American kids from bad old sheriffs like
me...I figured something must have raised your con-
sciousness about being Hispanic.''

''It was college. I mean, it wasn't like I didn't
know I was Hispanic before then. It was just...I was
sheltered. It was different when I went to U.T. There
wasn't my circle of friends. And I began to realize
how different I was. I wasn't Anglo, but I didn't fit
in with the Hispanic kids, either. It wasn't just the
language—obviously they spoke English, too. But I
didn't share any kind of background with them. Like
that *quinceañero* thing—I didn't have one. I didn't
even know what it was. I didn't have the same life
experiences. And I began to realize how much I had
missed, how I was cut off from this whole aspect of
myself. So I started reading. I took a class about
Mexican-American culture. And a minicourse about
the Latino movement. The more I studied it, the more
I got into it, the more I wanted to do something. You
know?''

Quinn nodded. "Sure. So is that when you decided to go to law school?"

Lisa nodded. "Yeah. I'd always been a good student, made good grades. But I didn't know what I wanted to do, really. Then, when I started looking at the typical Mexican-American experience in this country, the one I didn't have, I wanted to do something to help other Hispanics." She paused, then added honestly, "I felt guilty about having lived the kind of life I had, about not having had to face poverty and prejudice—I mean the worst thing that had ever happened to me was one time in the mall when this jerk told me I ought to go back where I came from." She giggled. "I was so clueless, I thought he meant University Park, where we lived. Anyway, it wasn't exactly like growing up in a *colonia* in the Valley."

"It's not anything to be ashamed of—it's only natural for your parents and your dad's parents to give their kids the best life they could. Who doesn't want that for their children?"

"Yeah. But in doing so they had denied their heritage, and that made me feel ashamed."

Lisa looked at him, thinking how strange it was that she was talking to this man about such things. She hadn't explained her tangle of feelings about her background to even her best friend, yet here she was telling a virtual stranger—and one who she would have said wouldn't have the slightest empathy for what she was talking about. She wasn't sure why it was—maybe it was the intent way he listened, his eyes on her, his body leaning slightly toward her. Was this how he encouraged criminals to confess their crimes?

"It's a funny thing, heritage," Quinn said. "Some people have a real need for it. Others...it doesn't seem to matter to them at all. Me—I like old things. It means a lot to me that I have something that my grandparents owned. If I go to East Texas, I look around at those farms and trees and houses and I think, 'This is where my ancestors came from.' It's like, somehow, it makes it part of me. But my sister Beth's not like that at all. Or Cory. He looks at a pie safe and thinks, 'What the hell is that old thing?' People are different. Maybe it just wasn't important to your father."

"Obviously not. But I wish that he had thought about the fact that it might be important to me." She shrugged. "But he's too nice a guy to get mad at him. And I can't dislike Anglos, either. I mean, my mother's Anglo and her family, and they're *my* family. Besides, it's pretty ungrateful, not to mention unrealistic, to be upset with your parents because they gave you a great life and protected you from poverty and prejudice."

"So you just felt guilty."

"Yeah. And I felt that I ought to give something to all those other people who hadn't had the same advantages I did. Law seemed to be the way to do that, and once I got started in it, I loved it. I realized it was exactly what I wanted to do with my life."

"So how come you didn't take Spanish in college?"

"I'd already gotten advanced placement in German. That's what I took in high school. So I signed up for the second year of German my freshman year. I didn't need another language. I thought about taking Spanish anyway, but…" She cast him a sideways glance. "I was always too embarrassed."

Quinn chuckled, and she frowned at him.

"You be quiet. It *was* embarrassing. I knew everybody would look at me and think I was taking it for an easy credit. Or if I didn't know things, then they would think I was stupid. And I didn't really consider how important it would turn out to be. After I interned at the P.D.'s office in Dallas, I realized I ought to learn it, but I was too busy in law school to take on a language course, too. I'd do it now, except there's no place to take it here. Not even a community college." She looked embarrassed again. "I got one of those computer language courses, actually, but it didn't do the trick. I think maybe after my year's up here, I'll go back to Austin and take an intensive course, one of those things they teach to company executives and diplomats, where they have to learn the language in two weeks or a month."

"When your year's up?" Quinn pounced on her words. "You mean you aren't planning to stay here?"

"In Hammond? Are you serious? No. I'm not planning to stay. I have a commitment to the THL for a year, and then I'm heading back to the city."

"Now why would you want to go and leave us? Are you telling me that you don't like it here?"

"Well...I guess I'm just a city girl."

"Why is that?"

"Movies, for one thing. Restaurants. Specialty stores. Things to do, things to see."

"Yeah, and traffic," Quinn countered. "Crime. Pollution. Lots of hurrying and scurrying. So many people around you, you can hardly breathe. Besides, there's lots of things to do and see here."

"Oh, yeah?" Lisa cocked an eyebrow at him.

"Yeah. You just haven't seen them. Somebody ought to introduce you to the joys of country life. I'd be happy to offer myself as a guide."

Lisa chuckled. "I don't really think I need one."

"Sure you do. See, the things to do in the country are more subtle, not so obvious."

"Like watching grass grow?"

"If you want, that can be fun, too. But I was thinking more like watching the sunset or maybe lying in the back of a pickup with a cooler full of beers and watching the stars."

"Doesn't sound very exciting."

He grinned at her, his red-brown eyes lighting in a devilish way. "Well, now, darlin', that depends on who you're with."

Lisa rolled her eyes. "I might have known you'd say that. But I was thinking about, I don't know, something a little livelier."

"There's dancing here in Hammond. And there

are restaurants. That one you were eating at last night is as good as any I ever went to in San Antonio.''

"It was good," Lisa agreed. "I was impressed. But I like a little variety."

"There's always the Dairy Queen." He grinned. "Okay, you do only have a few choices of restaurants between here and Angel Eye. But if you're really hankering for something else, San Antonio's not that far away. You can always go in for a spree at the mall or a movie and dinner."

"It seems to me like it would be easier to live there."

"I left Angel Eye when I was eighteen. I wanted to see something a lot bigger and fancier, too. I lived in Austin for three years and San Antonio for eight. But I came back here."

"But it's your home," Lisa pointed out. "You probably have family here and friends."

"Yeah. That's the whole point of a small town."

"But, see, I don't. My family and friends are back in Dallas."

"You've got a friend here now."

His tone was serious, unlike his usual bantering, and Lisa looked up, surprised, and found herself gazing into his eyes, warm and compelling, pulling her toward him. He touched the back of her hand where it lay on the table between them, moving with a feather's lightness over her hand and down onto her wrist. A shiver ran through Lisa. Friendship, she thought, was not at all what she was feeling.

And the thing was, she realized, she liked what

she was feeling. It was a new experience for her—
the sizzle of excitement at Quinn's touch, the frisson
of anticipation, mingling with a hint of danger, the
unaccustomed sense of standing on the edge of something unknown. Her relationships with men in the
past had tended to be warm rather than exciting, taking second place to school, her work, her goals. She
had always been sensible. With Quinn she felt anything but sensible.

He smiled at her as if he knew why she had with-
drawn and said only, "How about another drink?"

As it turned out, the second drink led to a pro-
longed dinner, finished up with coffee, and all the
time they talked, gliding from one topic to another.
In the past Lisa had sometimes had difficulty carrying on conversations with strangers, but with Quinn
it was amazingly easy. He was pleasant to talk to, a
surprisingly good listener, and he was able to con-
verse on a wide variety of topics. And if the conversation ever lagged, he had a ready supply of stories, ranging from his days as a cop in San Antonio
to his large and interesting family, with which to en-
tertain her. Underlying all their talk, like a vibrant
bass line, was the thrum of sexual attraction between
them, adding spice to every word, every gesture,
every smile.

It was over two hours later that they returned to
her office, where her car was parked. Quinn walked
with her to her car, insisting that he should follow
her home, despite her laughing assurance that she
was safe in Hammond.

"Don't you remember what you said about the lack of crime here?" Lisa asked, opening her car door and turning to face him.

"Ah, but a gentleman always walks a lady to her door," he replied. "How else would I get invited in for a cup of coffee?" He stood close, one hand on the roof of her car, the other hooked over her car door, hemming her in.

"We just had a cup of coffee," Lisa pointed out a little breathlessly.

"Well, then, maybe we can just smooch on your couch."

Lisa's eyes went involuntarily to his smooth, firm mouth. She thought about his kiss. Perhaps she ought to kiss him again, she thought, just to find out if that explosion of desire had been real and not just something that her mind had blown all out of proportion.

He cupped her chin in his hand, his thumb tracing the shape of her mouth. The touch of his rough skin against her lips made her tremble. She gazed into his eyes, and it felt as if she were falling into their depths.

"I don't…" she managed to murmur, and then his mouth was on hers, and all thought left her.

The heat and the magic were still there, blazing up like a wildfire as soon as his lips found hers. Her hands went up his chest and around his neck, holding on as desire rocked her to the core. She clung to him, the hard plane of his chest pressing against her soft breasts, her nipples hardening in response. Deep within her abdomen, heat blossomed, spreading out and consuming her as his mouth consumed hers.

One of his arms went around her waist, lifting her up and into him, the other went across the top of the open car door, shielding her back from the bite of the metal frame as he backed her up against it. A desperate sort of hunger seized Lisa, and she let out a little moan, her lips moving fervently against his. She wanted him, she ached for him, as she had never ached for any other man. She was all fire and hunger, molten and wild, taken over by an animalism that would shock her later when she recalled it. She wanted to be naked against Quinn, to feel his hands on her body. She wanted to wrap her legs around him and take him deep inside her, experiencing the full force of his strength and passion.

He tore his mouth from hers, kissing his way down the line of her throat. Her head fell back, and she shuddered out his name on a long breath. "Quinn…"

His hands ran down her body, slow and caressing, curving over her hips and back up. His lips returned to hers as though he could not get enough. Lisa twined her fingers through his hair, fingertips digging into his scalp as another shock of pleasure coursed through her.

If they had been at home, safe within the walls of her apartment, she was not sure what would have happened. She felt at that moment as though she had no will, no desire but to have him. But as it happened, a car turned onto the street a block down, its headlights falling on them in the dark, and she was brought back to the reality of where and what they were.

She pulled her head away, saying, "Wait. No...Quinn..."

She put her hands against his chest and pushed. He moved back reluctantly. His chest was heaving, his eyes glittering in the dark.

"What?" Quinn's voice came out a hoarse croak. "What's the matter?"

"A car."

There was a hoot from the car as it drove past slowly, and a rowdy voice called, "Hey, Deputy, you need some help?"

Quinn turned, grimacing. A young man was hanging out of the car, grinning back at them, and Quinn offered a good-natured wave of his hand. Lisa let out a moan and sank down onto the seat of her car, turned sideways.

"God, I hope that was no one I knew."

"They couldn't see you," Quinn reassured her. "All they saw was me, and they didn't know me— they thought I was a deputy."

He squatted down beside the car to be on a level with her. He took one of her hands in his, lacing his fingers through hers. He raised her hand to his lips. "Let me follow you home."

"No," Lisa replied decisively, pulling her hand from his grasp. "This was a mistake. A big mistake. I shouldn't have gone out for drinks with you, even. I should have known it would lead to this."

"Is this so terrible?"

"Of course it is. I was standing there making out with you on a public street. What if one of my clients had come by? Or some lawyer who knows us? I—we—well, it's wrong."

"Why? What's so wrong about it? I mean, I can see you don't want to be embarrassed by being caught like this, but…"

"You know why. I told you before. We are on opposite sides."

"What sides? You got your client out of jail. There isn't any case for there to be sides of."

"Yes, but there could be. What if you do find out something else about this thing you're working on and you arrest Benny, and I have to act as his attorney? I've been appointed defense counsel on several criminal cases since I've been in Hammond. What if I'm trying a case, and you turn up as a witness for the prosecution? And even if we never come into actual conflict on a case, in general, it just doesn't look good for a defense attorney to be chummy with the sheriff!"

"Is that what we were being? Chummy?" His eyes twinkled at her.

"Don't laugh at me. I'm serious."

"I'm sorry. I just naturally smile when I look at you. I like looking at you."

"Okay. You are a charmer, I'll admit that. You are doubtless devastating to all the females of this county. And surprisingly enough, I enjoyed your company tonight."

"Thanks—I think."

"If things were different, I would probably—but they aren't." She stopped and looked at him, setting her chin in a stubborn way. She realized that she sounded flustered and even ditzy, and it irritated her. She was supposed to be a cool, calm professional.

"You're tough. You know that?" he commented and rose with a sigh. "Tell you what, I'll follow you home, but I won't come in. I just want to make sure you get home safe. Call me old-fashioned. As for the rest of it…well, let's give it some time. Okay?"

Time? Time for what? But even as she thought the words, she knew what he intended—time for him to persuade her to do what he wanted. Quinn Sutton was not the kind of man who gave up easily. She supposed that she ought to argue with him about it, convince him that she had no intention of going to bed with him in the future either. But he was already moving away, going back to the sheriff's car, leaving her with little choice but to swing her legs into her own car, close the door, and drive away.

It was pointless to argue with him, anyway, she told herself as she drove to her apartment building and parked, then walked to her door. She turned as she went inside and saw his tan patrol car drive off.

Quinn, she knew, would just keep coming up with reasons why she was wrong. But she was certain that it would be disastrous to mix her personal life with her professional one, particularly when she was talking about someone she would always be at odds with. The only thing for her to do was to be strong-willed— not see him, not go out with him if he asked, not take his phone calls. She had to show him that she meant what she said. After a while, even Quinn would give up. There were all too many women out there who would be ecstatic to have Quinn Sutton turn his attention to them.

Lisa suppressed a twinge of irritation at that thought. She had no right to be jealous about Quinn Sutton. She was not going to date the man. She wasn't even going to see him again if she could help it. *And that was that.*

It took four days for Lisa to break her own rules.

She had not realized that it would be so difficult for her to be disciplined about the matter. She had thought that he might call her or drop by again, that it might be hard to avoid him long enough to get past the way she was feeling. But the fact of the matter was that *she* could not stop thinking about Quinn Sutton. She remembered their passion, their conversation, the way he looked. At all sorts of odd moments of the day, whenever her mind drifted away from whatever task was in front of her, Quinn would take over her thoughts. He didn't have to do a thing; her own mind and body had taken on the job.

She ploughed through the weekend, spending all of Saturday in San Antonio going to a movie and wandering through a mall, all the while plagued by thoughts of Quinn. She was drawn to a dress in the window of a store, simply made but devastatingly attractive and of a vivid blue color that she thought went particularly well with her pale olive complexion. She went inside and tried it on, all the while imagining what Quinn's face would register when he saw her in it.

Not that he would. She knew that. But she had bought the dress anyway, unable to resist it once she saw herself in the mirror. She would find an occasion to wear it, she told herself, even though it would not involve Quinn. It would be just as pretty.

Then she had driven home and thought depressing thoughts about the fact that she was in her apartment and settled for the night at ten o'clock on a Saturday evening.

Sunday was worse because she had nothing to do except putter around the apartment all day, attending to various beauty routines such as a masque and a manicure that she had been putting off for far too long. Unoccupied, her thoughts zeroed in on the sheriff. *Would there really be that much harm in dating him?* Before Benny, every one of her criminal cases had involved the Hammond Police Department, not the sheriff's office. The sheriff's office took care of the law enforcement for the much smaller population of the rest of the county, primarily Angel Eye, and most of their work was in the nature of traffic violations. Even if by chance someone in the sheriff's office was called in to testify on a case that she was involved in, it would in all probability be one of Quinn's deputies, not the sheriff himself. A sheriff generally did not spend much of his time doing ordinary patrolling. So the odds of her being in conflict with him on a case were small, really. And if one did arise, she knew, she could always withdraw from the case.

It wasn't as if the fact that she was dating the sheriff would influence her or what she did at work. Quinn was right; things were different in a little town; one was much more likely to mingle socially with people one faced in court, whether judges, police officers, or prosecuting attorneys. As long as she remained professional and kept a firm line between work and her personal life…

Lisa grimaced, exasperated at her own thoughts. Even if it were true that she could date the sheriff and continue with her criminal work without a conflict of interest, it was still foolish to do so. After all, she would be leaving here in ten months, as soon as her year was up, and it would be pointless to get involved with anyone before that happened. It would lead to nothing but unhappiness.

Besides, unhappiness was what lay in store for anyone who got involved with Quinn Sutton, she pointed out to herself. The man was charming, obviously far too skilled at captivating the opposite sex. Men like that were dangerously attractive, but incapable of any deep relationship with a woman. Her secretary had as much as said that about him. He was a womanizer, a ladies' man, the kind who enjoyed the hunt but never made a commitment. Clearly, dating him would only lead to heartache.

She realized the inconsistency of her arguments— she couldn't date him because she wouldn't be here long, but she couldn't date him because he would want only a short-term relationship—and that only irritated her more. By the time she went to sleep that night, she was thoroughly exasperated with herself.

The next afternoon, as she sat at her desk, she remembered that she had wanted to look up the deed to a property which one of her clients rented. She had thought about it early last week, then had put it aside as her workload had increased. She did not need the information any time soon, of course.

Still, she thought now, she would have to do it sometime. It might as well be today as a few days from now or next week. It would require a trip to the county courthouse, of course, where the records were kept, but...*oh, who was she kidding?* She knew she did not have to look at the records today. She was looking for an excuse to go to the county courthouse and perhaps run into Quinn.

Lisa leaned back in her chair and sighed, running her hands back into her hair and tugging at it until her scalp hurt. *Why did she keep thinking about the man?* She knew that she was acting like a schoolgirl, trying to manufacture excuses to "accidentally" see the sheriff again.

Quinn would see right through it, she told herself, after all her big talk about not seeing him again. It made her blush with embarrassment just to think about that slow, knowing smile of his. He would be sure that she hadn't meant anything she said, that she had simply been hoping that he would talk her out of her decision. *And why hadn't he called her, anyway? Was it that easy for him to give her up?*

She told herself that she was being an idiot, and she returned to her work, sternly stopping her thoughts every time they threatened to go astray. She made it through the day. But the next day, she finally gave up with a sigh and drove over to Angel Eye.

Telling herself that she probably would not even see him, she strode into the courthouse and went down to the basement to the county clerk's office, where she looked up the deed she had come to see. A few minutes later, she climbed the stairs to the first floor. She glanced around, then started toward the tall front doors, telling herself that she was not going to appear even more foolish by loitering around here, hoping that the sheriff would pop out of his office.

Feeling a trifle let down, she stepped out onto the front steps of the courthouse and looked down to see Quinn Sutton coming up them. He stopped, and a wide smile crossed his face—not the knowing smile she had imagined, but a smile of pure pleasure that made her heart flip-flop in her chest.

"Lisa!" he said, trotting up the last few steps to stand just below her, his face on a level with hers. "Well, you've made my day."

Lisa was aware that her smile was far too wide, but she could not seem to control it. "Hi. I, uh, had to check a deed at the county clerk's office."

"I've been thinking about you," he said.

"Really?"

"Yeah. Wondering if you would bite my head off if I called you."

"I hope I'm not that bad."

"Oh, you're not bad at all," he responded in a lazy drawl that made her blood heat.

She could feel a blush rising in her cheeks, and she looked away.

"So," he went on, "would you have talked to me if I'd called?"

"I guess we'll never know now, will we?" Lisa responded, realizing even as she said it that her manner was much too flirtatious. "I mean, well, you didn't, and I—of course I would have talked to you. But it still isn't a good idea. I mean, well, there's no point." Lisa stopped, wondering if she could possibly sound any more foolish.

"No point?"

"Yes. I mean…" Lisa took a firm grip on herself, managing a cool, even disinterested tone. "After all, ethically it's questionable. And I am going to be here for only a few more months. It would be silly to get involved with anyone. And you…"

"And me what?" he asked after she trailed to a halt.

"You…well, it would be pointless for you, too." She realized that she could hardly accuse him of being a womanizer, as if she wanted some long-term commitment from him.

"Well, what if we didn't think about all the heavy stuff, like where you're going to be in a year and whether we might get into opposing positions professionally and whatever you were going to say about me but realized would be impolite."

Her cheeks flamed with color. "No! Quinn, I didn't—oh, all right, I did. I was going to say that everyone says you bounce around from woman to woman, and half the women in town are in love with you."

Quinn chuckled. "Oh, I think that's an exaggeration. It's no more than a quarter of them. Come on, Lisa, haven't you figured out that small towns love to gossip? You can't trust half of what you hear. And if I have dated a lot…" He shrugged and smiled engagingly. "Well, maybe I just haven't found the right woman."

"See? That's what I'm talking about. Charming and fickle."

"You can't be charming without being fickle, too?"

"They go hand in hand, I've found." She squared her shoulders. "Look, Quinn, you and I both know that you are a hunter, the kind who likes the chase, and you are interested in me primarily because I have been resisting you. Once the chase is over, you get bored and disinterested."

"The answer to getting rid of me is obvious. Just let me catch you, and I'll be gone."

"I'm serious. Everything about you and me is wrong."

"How can that be true when I enjoy being around you so much? And don't tell me that it's more fun to be sitting in your office writing legal briefs than standing around flirting with me on the courthouse steps."

"Oh, really…" She turned and walked around him.

He pivoted, falling into step beside her. "Come on, admit it, weren't you hoping, at least a little bit, that you might run into me when you went to the records office?"

"I admit that you are fun," Lisa said grudgingly.

"Well, then, why don't we forget the other stuff and concentrate on that? I like to see you because it's fun, and you feel the same way. So we could go out sometime and have fun. That's all."

"It wouldn't be all."

"I tell you what, why don't you go with me to this family thing this weekend?" he asked. "Not a date—just a friend helping out a friend. I don't have anyone to go with me, and my family will be bugging me the whole time about why I didn't bring someone. It's in the afternoon, so that's not like a date, right?"

"I guess." Lisa cast him a sideways glance. It scared her a little how much she wanted to agree to go with him.

"So could we agree to do that? Just a friendly thing, non-threatening, no commitment…"

The problem, she knew, was that there was little likelihood that she could be around Quinn for any length of time, and have it not involve something more than friendship. Both the times she had been with him before had ended in a kiss. *But what would be so terrible about that? Maybe a little passion was just what she needed in her life.*

"Well, I suppose there wouldn't be any harm..." she began.

"Great. I'll pick you up at one, Saturday afternoon. It starts at two, but I have to be there early. I'll pick you up about one, say?"

"I live in the Windemere Apartments," Lisa replied and began to give him directions.

Quinn grinned. "No need. I know where they are. I followed you home the other night. Remember? I'll see you Saturday then."

"Wait. What is this family thing? What should I wear? I mean, is it a picnic or what?"

He grinned. "No. It's not a picnic. Wear something nice. It's my brother Daniel's wedding."

Chapter 5

It was impossible, Lisa thought, looking at herself in the full-length mirror on her closet door. She should not be going to a family wedding with Quinn. She had told him so as soon as he'd said what the event was, and she had called him at work two days later to re-assert the absolute inappropriateness of the whole thing.

"It's ludicrous," she had argued. "I barely know you, and I don't know anyone else in your family at all. I don't belong at a family wedding. It's too—"

"Too what?"

Well, too intimate, that's what, too weighted in meaning. "It's a family occasion," she had said instead. "You shouldn't take a casual date to it."

"Why not?"

"Because it is something serious and meaningful

to the people who are getting married. It's an occasion when they want their family and friends around, not complete strangers.''

''They don't mind if I bring somebody. They expect me to. Look, the wedding's not going to be big. It's the second time around for both of them. But half the county will be at the reception.'' At her pointedly raised eyebrow, he continued. ''Okay, maybe not half. But a whole lot of people. My family has lived here forever, and Daniel's new wife is the local vet. They know everybody. It's a big celebration. And if I show up without a date, my brothers will tease the hell out of me all afternoon, and my father and sister will worry because they think I ought to be doing some serious wife-shopping.''

''And I'm supposed to be a possible wife?'' Lisa's voice slid upward rapidly.

''Now, don't get your knickers in a twist. They aren't going to try to hog-tie you and drag you to the altar. But if I can't even manage to bring somebody to the wedding, they will be sure I'm on my way to old codger-hood.''

He had gone on persuasively, ''It won't be bad, darlin'. I promise you. My family hasn't eaten anybody in years now. You'll like my sister Beth—people always do. And, hey, she's married to a big Hollywood director, so you'll get to meet somebody famous.''

''Are you serious?''

''Sure. Now why would I make something like that up?''

He had then gone on to relate the story of his pregnant sister's first meeting with Jackson Prescott on the side of the road, where she was stranded and going into labor, and his frantic drive to the hospital with her, followed by the comedy of errors that had had all the Sutton males ending up in a brawl in the hospital with Prescott. By the time he was through, Lisa had been laughing so hard her sides hurt, and she had given up her attempt to reason with him.

Now, the day of the event, Lisa was still certain that it was a bad idea for her to accompany Quinn to his brother's wedding. Attending a wedding with someone implied a certain closeness, an intimacy that was not the case with them. It made her feel uneasy. His family was bound to get the wrong impression, and so would the other guests. But, looking at herself in the mirror, wearing the blue dress that she had bought last weekend in San Antonio, she could not bring herself to back out of it. The dress was perfect for a wedding, its wonderfully strappy and enticing back covered demurely by a short jacket, and she was longing to wear her new acquisition. Besides, it set off her skin and her figure so well that she knew, down deep, that she was eager to let Quinn see her in it.

His reaction a few minutes later when she opened the door to his knock was everything she could have hoped for. His eyes widened, and dark reddish light flared up in them. He straightened from his lounging position and stepped forward, his eyes running down her body appreciatively.

"Well," he said after a moment, "already this is turning out to be better than I thought."

"You had low expectations?" Lisa asked lightly, mentally observing that Quinn did not look at all shabby himself. For the first time since she had known him, he was dressed in something other than his uniform: a black tuxedo and white pleated shirt with a conservative black cummerbund and bow tie. It was possible, she thought, that he looked even better dressed this way.

"No. Just not a good enough imagination. I knew you'd look good enough to turn me inside out. I just didn't know how far."

Lisa glanced down to hide the involuntary spurt of desire that flared in her at the look on his face. Her eyes fell on his feet, clad in black boots.

She smiled. "Dress boots?"

"Yes, ma'am. You are, after all, in ranch country."

"I see. Does this mean that you are going to be in the wedding?"

"Just an usher. It's a small wedding, so Dan's having only his son stand up with him. We three brothers got delegated usher duty. 'Course, that's better than Beth—she has to dish out stuff at the reception."

They were among the first to arrive at the small white stucco church. When they walked in, they found four other men, dressed in tuxedos and all similarly tall and dark-haired, lounging about in the center aisle at the front of the church. Lisa's gaze went immediately to their feet, all clad in black cowboy boots, and she smiled.

"Hey, Quinn." One of the men glanced up and saw them and started toward them.

"Cater." Quinn's gaze went to the others. "Daniel, how you doing?"

"Okay if I don't throw up." One of the men answered him, his dark eyes twinkling.

"I'm keeping an eye on him." This was said by the youngest and tallest of the men. His hair was thick and black, longer and shaggier than the other men's hair. He was stick-thin in the way of teenage boys who have grown too fast to carry any bulk on them, but the bony planes of his face were very handsome, and Lisa suspected that he was the heartthrob of every girl in school.

Lisa and Quinn walked up the aisle as the men began to amble toward them. The first to reach them was the one Quinn had called Cater. About Quinn's height, he was black-haired, with startling, deep-blue eyes. He was the most handsome of the brothers, Lisa thought, and also the most polished and sophisticated-looking, the only one who did not appear slightly uncomfortable in his formal suit.

"Lisa, this is Cater, one of my brothers. He's the writer."

Cater took the hand she offered, smiling at her, and Lisa thought that this family of men was probably lethal to the female heart. Quinn introduced the other brothers, first Daniel, the groom, whose tanned, slightly weather-beaten face and callused hands spoke of his years working outdoors. If she remembered what Quinn had told her correctly, he raised horses for a living and was considered one of the best in the state at training cutting horses. The young man was, as she had suspected, Daniel's son James, whom Quinn introduced with pride as being a freshman film student at UCLA. He had flown in the day before from Los Angeles to attend the wedding. The fourth man was Cory, tall with the same rangy build as the others, and obviously the youngest of the brothers, probably in his early twenties. His hair color was medium brown, and his eyes were hazel. He resembled Quinn the most in the face, but without the faint touch of hardness that characterized Quinn's expression when he wasn't smiling or joking. He, she was told, was a senior at the University of Texas.

"Well, I can understand why Quinn's been talking so much about you now, ma'am," Cory said with a grin reminiscent of Quinn's own.

"Don't even think about flirting with her," Quinn warned him.

"Come on, Quinn, how could we not flirt with a woman who looks like this?" Cory replied reasonably. He glanced past Lisa, and his face lit up.

"Hey! How's my boy?"

Lisa turned to see that a couple had entered the church. The man was handsome and well-dressed and bore no resemblance to the Sutton men. The woman was tall and attractive, with hair the color of Quinn's, and Lisa knew that this must be his sister, Beth. The man carried in his arms a toddler who, upon seeing the men, held out both arms, opening and closing his fists eagerly.

"Cowy!" he cried, smiling. "Cowy."

Cory went to them, reaching out for the toddler, and the little boy practically flew into his arms. Cory lifted him above his head in a way obviously familiar to both of them, and the youngster went off into a paroxysm of giggles.

"Beth, I want you to meet Lisa Mendoza," Quinn said, introducing them as he went to his sister and wrapped one arm around her shoulders, hugging her.

Beth greeted Lisa with warm enthusiasm. "Sit with us while Quinn's ushering," she said, "and I can find out all about you. Quinn is miserable with details. Cory will keep Joseph occupied the entire time, I can promise, so he won't bother us."

She linked her arm through Lisa's and swept her up the aisle to a row near the front, while her husband stayed to greet the circle of men. Warm and vivacious, Beth kept up a lively chatter that smoothed away whatever nerves Lisa had felt on meeting Quinn's family, and interspersed her comments with a spate of questions, but all in such a charming way that Lisa could not be offended by her curiosity.

"Quinn and I are closest in age," she told Lisa. "We were best of friends, even though we fought all the time, too. Red hair, you see." She made a gesture toward her wildly curling mass of hair. "He's got quite a temper—oh, but he's never rough or mean, though, and he always gets over it quickly. You just

wait a little bit, and Quinn'll cool down. Have you
known him long?''

''No, actually we just met about ten days ago, and
I confess that I feel a little awkward coming to the
wedding,'' Lisa replied. ''I'm afraid your family
must wonder why I'm intruding.''

''Heavens, no. Quinn always has a date to every-
thing.'' She paused, looking a trifle uneasy. ''Wait.
I didn't mean that the way it came out. It's not that
Quinn is—is—''

''A womanizer?'' Lisa proffered.

Beth's eyes rounded, and she looked stricken.
''Oh, no, you mustn't think that. Quinn likes women,
but he doesn't play fast and loose with them. I mean,
he does date a lot, but he, he—oh, dear, I'm just
making it sound worse, aren't I? Quinn will kill me.
What I mean is, maybe he is a bit of a flirt, but it's
not serious most of the time. You know? And it's
not as if he isn't capable of a deep commitment. I'm
sure of that. He is a very loyal person, and his emotions are deep. I—''

Lisa smiled. ''Don't worry. You haven't smashed
my illusions about Quinn. We aren't really dating,
and I don't expect some sort of big relationship with
Quinn. Actually, we met because of our work, and
we're just…friends.''

Beth looked at her a little skeptically. ''Well, I
can't speak for you, of course, but as for Quinn—I
think he's interested in you as something more than
a friend. This morning when he and I were together,
you were all he talked about.''

"Really? I—well—"

"You know," Beth went on confidentially, "what I was really trying to say is that even though Quinn has always dated a lot of different women, I think it's because he hasn't found the right one. He's a very loving person, and when he falls in love, I think he'll fall really hard. And he won't change. I'm sure of that. Right now…I think it's not that he's fickle. I think it's that he's—maybe *guarded* is the right word."

"Guarded? Against what?"

Beth shrugged. "I don't know. Hurt, maybe. I don't know if he told you, but Quinn was a cop for several years in San Antonio. It changed him. After he came back from there, he wasn't as uncomplicated as he had been before. There was a look in his eyes that hadn't been there before, and he wasn't—he wasn't as easy to be close to."

"It hardened him?"

"I think so. In some ways. I mean, he's still fun, he's still charming. Everyone loves Quinn. But he's not as open, as trusting. I don't know what happened. I don't know if it was the kind of things he saw as a policeman or—or if something else happened to him. But it's been since then, I think, that he's been so casual about dating, no long-term relationships. He wasn't as much like that when he was younger." She paused, then added tentatively, "I hope I haven't done anything to make you like him less. Quinn's the best. I should learn to keep my mouth shut more."

"No. You haven't done anything wrong," Lisa reassured her with a smile. "I like Quinn. But I'm like him in that I'm not really interested in a long-term relationship, either. I'm going to be here for less than a year, and it's best if I don't get involved with anyone seriously."

"Oh." Beth looked disappointed, but a moment later, when she learned that Lisa was from Dallas and planning to return there, she launched into a pleasant, bubbly conversation about that city, where she had lived for several years herself.

People had been gradually filling the seats around them as they had talked, and their conversation had grown more and more hushed as a consequence. Beth's husband had come to sit with them, carrying the baby Joseph, who was less than pleased that his companion, Cory, was seating guests instead of playing with him, and he kept them all occupied for several minutes with his squirming attempts to get back to his uncle.

An older man slid into the seat on the other side of Jackson Prescott, and Beth introduced him to Lisa as their father, Marshall Sutton. Even without the introduction, Lisa felt sure she would have known who he was—though his black hair was liberally streaked with white, he was so much an older version of Quinn's brother Daniel that he could hardly have been anyone other than the patriarch of the Sutton clan.

A few minutes later, the music started and the wedding began. The wedding did not appear to Lisa to be particularly small, as almost three-fourths of the chapel was filled. The bride, Lisa saw, was a breathtakingly beautiful blond woman, tall and slender with a patrician look. It was a little hard to reconcile her elegant appearance with the fact that Quinn had told Lisa she was a veterinarian.

The ceremony was simple and short, but beautiful as well. Beside Lisa, Beth had tears rolling down her cheeks as the couple said their vows. Quinn, who had come to sit down on the other side of Lisa when his ushering duties were done, took Lisa's hand in his, his finger intertwining with hers. She glanced at him, but he was not looking at her, only watching his brother and his bride, a faint smile on his lips. Feeling her gaze, he turned to Lisa, and his smile broadened. Leaning close to her, he placed a brief kiss against her temple.

Lisa closed her eyes, her throat suddenly tight, and she grasped his hand a little tighter. It was foolish, she told herself, to feel emotion at the marriage of people who were complete strangers to her, but she could not help it. There was something so beautiful and romantic in the moment that it swept her up in it, and she was glad that she had come, glad to be sitting beside Quinn, his hand warm around hers.

Later, at the reception, she saw that Quinn had been right in saying that the wedding was small, at least in comparison to the huge crowd that spread over the wide front verandah of the house and across the circular drive and lawn, wrapping around the house even to the back, where the swimming pool

lay. Tables and chairs had been placed all around the
pool, as they had on the front porch and under canopies on the lawn, and water lilies floated in silent
elegance on the surface of the water. Brightly striped
canopies shaded the food and guests, as well as a
band on a raised temporary platform. The food was
delicious, catered by the Moonstone Café, and it was
there in abundance, as was champagne, bubbling out
of a fountain.

Lisa ate and drank champagne and danced, mostly
with Quinn, but also at least once with each of his
brothers. Even his father took her out on the dance
floor one time, expertly guiding her through a country waltz. She met so many people she couldn't remember all their names, and they all talked to her in
that open, friendly way that was so common in the
country. She met Daniel's bride, who, with the flush
of happiness in her cheeks, was even prettier close
up and far less cool and reserved than her ice-
princess beauty made her appear. Antonia introduced
her to Rita Delgado, a plump, pretty woman in her
thirties who worked at the veterinary clinic with Antonia and was her best friend and matron of honor.
Rita in turn introduced her to her cousin, Lena, who,
it turned out, was the night dispatcher for the sheriff's office.

Lena beamed and patted her on the arm. "I've
been dying to meet you. You're the one doesn't
speak Spanish, right? Everybody else got to see you
that day but me."

"Oh, no," Lisa groaned. "Did he tell everyone about that?"

"Who?"

"Quinn."

"It wasn't Quinn. I heard it from my mother. Mama's a cousin to Benny Hernandez's grandmother, and it was her who told my mother."

"Nothing's a secret in this town," said Quinn's low voice in her ear.

Lisa whirled to find Quinn standing behind her, a beer in his hand and a smile on his face. He slipped his arm around her from behind, fitting his body to hers. She could feel his heat and the thump of his heart in his chest, and where his arm wrapped around her, her flesh tingled with awareness and desire.

"Yeah," Lena agreed. "Everything gets out sooner or later. Especially to me."

"Oh. I see. Yes, I am the one who doesn't know Spanish."

"She's never even made tamales at Christmas, Lena," Quinn offered.

From the horrified look on the dispatcher's face, Lisa presumed that this must amount to heresy.

"*Verdad?* No. You must do something about that. Come to our house on Christmas Eve this year and we'll show you. My *abuelita* gets the whole family in there working, and we make enough to feed half the town."

"That's true," Quinn agreed. "She always brings me a bunch of 'em." He grinned and shot a significant look at Lena. "Otherwise I might have to find a new night dispatcher."

"Oh, you…" Lena dismissed this threat with the contempt it deserved. "I mean it, Quinn, you bring this girl over to the house this year. We might even let you help."

Lisa smiled and agreed, warmed by their friendliness. Maybe there *were* benefits to living in a little town, she thought.

"Care for another dance?" Quinn murmured, his breath tickling her ear and sending shivers through her.

Lisa nodded, leaning into him, and with a wave of the hand to Lena and Rita, he led her away to the driveway, where the bandstand had been set up and couples were dancing. The music was slow and dreamy, and Lisa melted into Quinn's arms. He was a good dancer, and though she had not known any country-western dances before today, she was rapidly learning them under his tutelage. But this dance, as slow and languid as summer heat, required no steps, only the sway and turn of two bodies matched together. His arm was around her, his hand cupped around her hipbone on the opposite side, and Lisa found her head resting naturally against his chest. She closed her eyes, letting the music take her.

When the dance ended, she heard Quinn's long exhalation of breath, felt it beneath her cheek. Reluctantly she stepped back, looking up at him. Quinn's mahogany eyes were filled with heat, and color lay along the ridges of his cheekbones.

"Come on," he said, a trifle hoarsely, linking his hand with hers and turning away. Lisa went along with him as he strolled across the yard to the side door. He opened the door and stepped into the kitchen, a hive of activity under the direction of Elizabeth Morgan.

Nodding toward Elizabeth, he sidestepped two workers and took Lisa through the dining room and into the entry hall. The inside of the house was almost empty except for the workers in the kitchen.

"What are we doing?" Lisa asked as Quinn walked around the stairs and down the hall.

"This." Quinn stopped beside a door tucked underneath the stairs and opened it.

Lisa looked inside. It was a narrow room with a ceiling that rose as the stairs went up. There was an old easy chair to one side of the door.

"This is where I used to hide out," Quinn explained. "I don't know why, but it was always sort of my room. I put the chair in here and a lock on the door, and I'd come in here and read or talk on the phone."

"It's cute," Lisa said, stepping inside. "Like a little playhouse."

Quinn followed her, pulling the string that turned on the overhead bulb. "I was just thinking out there how much I wanted to be alone with you, so..."

He closed the door behind them and slid the bar lock in place.

"Oh, really?" Lisa raised her eyebrows in what she hoped was a cool questioning, but her heart immediately started to hammer and anticipation rose within her.

"Yeah, really," Quinn replied, taking a step closer and gazing down into her eyes. "The whole time we were dancing, this is all I could think about."

His arms went around her, lifting her up into him, and he bent his head to kiss her. Heat flared between them, swift and fiery, as if a match had been set to kerosene. Lisa wrapped her arms around his neck, clinging to him. He kissed her deeply, his tongue sliding into her mouth, hungry and demanding. She met it eagerly, her own tongue twining around his in a passionate dance. She, too, had been daydreaming about this moment.

Quinn's arms loosened around her, but only so that his hands were free to move over her. She had abandoned the jacket of her dress some time earlier in the heat of the dancing, and now his hands slid over her bare back, slipping beneath the tangle of straps that crisscrossed it. His fingers were rough against her satiny skin, and the contrast stirred them both. His other hand roamed downward to her hips, curving over them, fingers digging into her buttocks.

Scrunching up the material of her skirt in his hands, he reached at last the bare flesh of her thigh. Lisa trembled at his touch, a hot ache blossoming in her abdomen. She wanted more than this, so much more that it was almost frightening. Her breasts were full and sweetly aching, longing for his touch, her nipples hardening. She moved against him, unconsciously rubbing her body against him, and he shuddered, a low moan escaping his throat.

He tore his lips from her mouth, raining kisses over her face and down her throat. His arm went around her back, supporting her, as Lisa leaned back. His other hand came up to cup her breast, exploring its softness through the material of her dress. He felt the thrust of her nipple against the cloth, and he cursed under his breath, frustrated by the barrier that kept what he wanted from him. He wanted to rip the cloth away, to taste her flesh, to take the hot, hard bud of her nipple into his mouth. Instead his hand slid down and up under the hem of her dress, gliding caressingly up her bare thigh, drawn as if by a magnet to the heat centered between her legs.

His fingers touched the silk of her panties, wet now with the moisture of her passion. Lisa moaned, her breath coming in hard, fast pants. Gently he explored her, teasing and caressing, as his mouth returned to take hers hungrily. He was hard and pulsing, almost desperate to take her.

There was the sound of footsteps on the tile entryway, followed by feet running lightly up the steps above their heads. Then there was the sound of a woman's voice calling Antonia's name, followed by more steps on the stairs.

Quinn pulled away from Lisa with a muffled oath. "Damn it! We can't do this here. I didn't mean to— I just couldn't bear it any longer. I had to sneak a kiss."

He turned away, running his hands back through

his hair and struggling for control. Lisa hastily pulled down her rucked-up skirt and took a step backward, too.

"I guess we can't leave until the bride and groom do," Quinn mused gloomily.

"Probably not," Lisa agreed a little breathlessly. "I mean, your being family."

"Damn family," Quinn added ungraciously.

They waited for a few more minutes, letting their blood cool and smoothing their hair and clothes. Finally, Quinn unlocked the door and peeked outside, then opened it wider and stepped out into the hall. Lisa followed on his heels as he went down the hall and out the back door into the pool area. It was filled with people, and Lisa hoped they didn't look too obvious. Carefully walking apart, they strolled around the pool and the house to the punch table, hoping that a cool drink might quench some of the heat lingering inside them.

It seemed to take forever for the bride to emerge from the house, having changed into a different, more casual dress. More time passed while she threw her bouquet and the newly married couple said good-bye to their family and friends and drove off. Lisa smiled until her mouth ached and avoided looking at Quinn. The moment of decision would be coming soon, she knew, and she didn't know what to do. What she wanted, with a deep, physical ache, was to go home with Quinn and take him up to her bed. But now that she was more or less in control of her senses again, she did not think that that would be a prudent thing to do.

Their having spent an afternoon together did not change any of the factors that made a relationship between them an unwise thing. He was still the sheriff; she was still leaving in less than a year; he specialized in short, casual relationships; and she was not a casual sort of person. They were anything but an ideal match. Besides, she simply did not fall into bed easily with any man. She never had. Of course, she had to admit to herself, she had never wanted so badly to fall into bed with any other man she had dated.

Quinn was different. The feelings he aroused in her were incendiary. But that, she knew, did not mean that it was necessarily right for her to give in to those feelings.

She was still pondering the problem when Quinn came up to her and slipped his hand around her arm. ''I think we can finally leave.''

It still took several minutes of goodbyes to Quinn's family and other wedding guests before they were able to walk down the long driveway to where Quinn's white pickup was parked. They got in and turned around, setting off down the road to the highway, along with a number of other guests. Neither of them spoke much. Lisa glanced at Quinn a time or two, wondering what he was thinking. She wondered if he was as unsure as she about what was going to happen when they reached her apartment.

She could resolve the issue, of course, by simply

not inviting him in, but that would be rude and he would probably take it to mean she didn't like him, which was obviously not the case. Or she could invite him in and then discuss the issue with him, but the problem with that was that when she was around Quinn, discussion was likely to slide right into passion in no time at all. Of course, she could also toss aside all her usual prudence and foresight and practicality and just let what would happen, happen. The thought made her a little uneasy, but it was also very enticing.

They drove through the little town of Angel Eye and took the highway toward Hammond. Just past Angel Eye, Quinn's cell phone began to ring. Cursing, he dug it out of the cup-holder where he had placed it and answered with a terse, "Yeah?"

He listened without saying anything for some time, then asked a few quick questions, ending with, "I'll be there in a minute."

Quinn hung up and looked over at Lisa. "That was Ruben. I—I'm sorry. I have to go somewhere."

"Okay." Worry stirred in Lisa at his expression. "What is it? Is something the matter?"

"Red Klingman just found a dead body on his ranch."

Chapter 6

For a long moment, Lisa could do nothing but stare at Quinn. "What? Who?"

He shook his head. "I don't know anything more than that. Ruben called me as soon as he heard. He's already sent a patrol car out to secure the scene, and he's called the coroner." He paused, then said, "It's off this highway a little ways. It'd be faster if I stopped on the way instead of taking you home first. Would you mind?"

"No. It's all right."

"I hate to ask you, but...well, I'm the only one here who's actually been on a homicide scene before. Phil's an okay kid, but if it turns out to be murder, I want to make sure that the crime scene isn't contaminated."

"Homicide? Here? You really think it is?"

He shrugged. "If it is, it's the first one since I've been sheriff. But I don't have any way of knowing yet. It could have been an accident or a suicide, too."

The thought of any sort of death on this lovely day was hard to accept, but homicide seemed almost beyond the realm of possibility. *In Angel Eye?* It was just a small, sleepy, quaintly named town, like hundreds of other little towns in Texas. It seemed absurd that something as grim as homicide could happen here.

Lisa wrapped her arms around herself, feeling suddenly chilled despite the pleasant October warmth of the day.

Quinn turned off the highway onto a smaller road, and after a few minutes, he made yet another turn onto a hard-packed dirt road. He followed this for a few minutes, rattling across a cattle guard, then driving slowly and looking searchingly out the window. Finally he saw what he was looking for: the tracks of a truck leaving the road and striking out along what seemed little more than a narrow trail.

Eventually they could see a dark green pickup truck ahead of them, parked in the middle of an empty field. Ominously, two or three big black birds circled in the air a short distance from the truck. A middle-aged man in a cowboy hat was sitting on the back of the truck bed, his legs dangling off the end. He cradled a shotgun in the crook of one arm.

Lisa sucked in a sharp breath. Beside her Quinn stiffened a little, but he said only. "It's okay. I know Red."

He stopped the car some distance from the truck, and Lisa noticed that he reached down underneath the seat and pulled out a handgun, which he checked and stuck in his belt at the small of his back. The man jumped off the back of the truck and started toward them, carrying the shotgun pointing unthreateningly down at the ground.

"Hey, Quinn," he said as he drew near the truck. "Sorry you got called out today. It's your brother's wedding, isn't it?"

"Yeah. But it was over anyway." Quinn spoke casually, but his eyes never left the other man, and he opened the door and stepped out of the truck to meet him.

"Hell of a thing to find," the other man said. Now that he was close, Lisa could see that his face was pale under his rancher's tan, almost a greenish hue. "I figured I had a dead cow when I saw those buzzards circling, so I drove over to see." He shook his head, obviously remembering the moment when he had seen that the dead body had not been a cow. "I been sittin' here shootin' off the gun every once in a while to keep the birds off it."

"Thanks, Red." Quinn glanced toward the vultures, still drifting through the air. "I guess with all the people that'll be here soon, they won't be lighting any more."

"Yeah." The other man glanced into the cab of Quinn's pickup and saw Lisa. "Oh. Hello, ma'am." He politely doffed his hat to her. "I didn't realize you were there. Sorry."

Lisa smiled at him, relieved to have learned the reason he was carrying a gun. "Hello."

"Did you recognize him, Red?" Quinn asked now.

The rancher grimaced, looking sick. "Lord, no, I couldn't even stomach gettin' close enough to look in his face. There's a fearsome stench. It was clear he was dead. Looks like a Mexican, that's all I could tell."

"Male?"

"Yeah. Looked like."

"Well, I guess I better go look at it," Quinn said.

"You want me to show you?" Red asked unenthusiastically.

"Nah, I can find it easy enough with those birds. As soon as one of my deputies gets here, he can take your statement, and you can go on home."

"Sure thing."

Quinn opened the door of the truck and leaned in to say to Lisa, "You stay here, okay? I want to keep the scene as clear as possible."

"Are you kidding?" Lisa looked at him with horror. "I have no intention of going anywhere near it."

He gave her a faint smile. "Wish I didn't have to."

She watched as Quinn turned and walked away, past Klingman's dusty green pickup and on toward the spot the vultures circled. He reached in his back pocket and pulled out a handkerchief as he went and held it to his nose. Lisa looked away, feeling slightly sick.

"Hell of a job," Red Klingman commented, watching Quinn, too.

"It must have been a shock, finding it."

The man nodded. "Yeah. I was sure glad Melanie wasn't with me. That's the missus."

They began to talk, more to distract their minds from the thought of what Quinn was examining than from any desire to have a conversation. Before long, a tan sheriff's car pulled up beside them, and a young deputy got out. He spoke to Klingman, then walked off to join Quinn.

When he and Quinn returned a few minutes later, the deputy looked considerably paler than he had when he arrived, and the freckles across the bridge of his nose stood out in stark contrast. By this time, another deputy had pulled up in a patrol car, and a Suburban had arrived, containing a man with a medical bag, who Lisa presumed must be the county coroner. The men shook hands all around, and Quinn set Deputy Padilla to taking Red Klingman's statement. Then he walked over to her side of the car, his face set in grim lines.

"Lisa, I'm sorry. It looks like I'm going to be here awhile. Will it be all right if Phil drives you home? I need to stay and oversee everything."

"Sure. I understand," Lisa reassured him.

So the young deputy drove her home in the patrol car, doing his best to appear less shaken by the crime scene than he obviously was. Lisa was glad to be away from the scene, even though she had not witnessed the obviously gruesome sight of the body.

Just the knowledge of it was more than enough for her imagination.

Lisa showered as soon as she got home, as if she could somehow wash away the experience, then curled up in an old robe on the couch and spent the evening watching television. Most of the time it served well enough to take her mind off what had happened, but she found her thoughts still straying now and again to the empty field and the chilling circling of the buzzards overhead. It must have been awful for that poor rancher to have stumbled upon it. She wondered if it had in fact been a homicide victim or if it was just some poor soul who had had an accident out in the middle of nowhere. That thought was disturbing enough; in fact, none of the options were good—suicide was a terrible end, as well.

She tried to turn her thoughts in another direction, going back to this afternoon and the happiness of the wedding and reception. That was something of a mental minefield, as well, though, for she kept remembering how wonderful it had felt to be in Quinn's arms and how uncertain she was about what to do about it.

It was after eleven when she finally got up to turn out the lights and go to bed. Just as she clicked off the remote, there was a knock on the front door. She jumped, clamping her teeth shut on a little shriek. Willing herself to be calm and mature, she went to the door and looked out the peephole. Quinn Sutton stood outside.

She opened the door quickly. "Quinn!"

"I'm sorry. I know it's late. I just, ah, wanted to make sure you got home okay. That you were all right."

He had obviously gone home and showered. He was wearing jeans and an old T-shirt, and his short hair curled damply. He smiled a little and added candidly, "Actually, I mostly wanted to see you."

"Sure. Come on in." Lisa stepped back so that he could enter the apartment.

"Sorry. I hope it's not too late."

"No, it's fine." Lisa refrained from adding that she was far more delighted than she probably should be to see him. "You want a beer?"

"That'd be great." Quinn flopped down on the sofa with a sigh and leaned back. Lisa went to the refrigerator and returned with a bottle of beer and a glass.

"Bottle's fine," he said, taking it and twisting off the cap. "Man! I'm sorry you had to see that."

"I didn't really see anything," Lisa pointed out and sat down at the other end of the couch. "Have you been out there all evening?"

He nodded. "Most of it. I went home and changed afterward. Figured you sure wouldn't want to see me the way I was." He let out a long breath, closing his eyes. "I hate this stuff."

"Death?"

"Yeah. Especially useless death."

"Was he murdered?"

"I don't know. Dr. Drachman couldn't tell from

examining the corpse. It wasn't anything immediately apparent. We've sent the body to the state M.E.'s office in Austin.''

"Do you know who it was?''

He shook his head. "No idea. He definitely looked Hispanic. Usually, you find a corpse like that, no ID, out in the middle of nowhere, Hispanic, you figure it's probably an illegal.''

"An alien?''

"Yeah. It happens a lot. They pay money to some guy, a 'coyote,' to get them across the border, and then he'll abandon them, just leave them in the desert to make it or die. Just a few weeks ago there was a story like that in Arizona, fifteen or twenty Mexican nationals dying out in the desert. Or they'll stuff some huge number in a truck, and a bunch of them die of the heat and dehydration.''

"How awful.''

"It's an awful business. I mean, what kind of person would take money from people like that, people who are so desperate they're paying him their last peso to get across the border, and then just leave them to die?''

"I don't know.'' Lisa moved closer to him, drawn by the pain in his voice, and took his hand. He intertwined his fingers through hers and gave her a small smile.

"Aren't you glad I came here to dump that on you?''

"I don't mind. I'm glad you came,'' Lisa answered honestly. Charming as Quinn normally was, there was something even more appealing to him now, raw and honest, vulnerable to the pain of his job.

"So you think that's what happened to this man? He was an illegal alien that got abandoned by his guide?"

"Could be. It has the markings of it. Only thing is, we're pretty far from the border for it. Things like this usually happen in the Valley. This is a pretty long way to have walked from the Rio Grande. Odds are he would already have succumbed to the heat and dehydration long before he got here. So...maybe it's something else. Maybe he's not an illegal. Maybe he's just a guy who somehow got lost out in the country. I've heard of people dying from exposure and being not all that far from a road, but they got so turned around, they never realized how close they were."

"But it's odd, not having any ID," Lisa mused.

"Yeah. It's real odd. A woman maybe has hers in her purse and loses that as she's getting dehydrated and delirious, stumbling around. But most guys carry their ID in a wallet in their pants. This guy had nothing in his pockets but lint."

"So you're suspicious."

"Yeah. I mean, it could turn out that he left it in his car or something, that his car broke down and for some stupid reason he decided to strike out across the open country instead of sticking to the road. But I think it's unlikely. Nor does it look like suicide— no ID, no note, no wound. Who kills himself by hik-

ing out in the semi-desert and waiting to die? I won't
know anything until we get the M.E.'s report, but
I'm assuming murder.''

"I'm sorry. It's a nasty way to end your brother's
wedding day.''

"It's a nasty way to end any day. Damn.'' He
leaned forward, resting his elbows on his legs, beer
bottle dangling from one hand. "I was hoping I'd
gotten away from that smell forever. I came back
here to Angel Eye to get rid of it. Now here it is,
cropping up in a little place like this.''

"I guess evil can happen anywhere.''

"I was a cop in San Antonio for seven years. I
can't tell you how many dead people I had to deal
with. Car wrecks, suicides, accidents, shootings,
stabbings. It affects you—the way you think, the way
you look at people, the way you live. I saw things
that would turn my stomach. Women—children—
killed by the person who was supposed to love
them.'' He looked over at her. "You don't want to
hear this stuff.''

"I do if you need to talk about it,'' Lisa replied.

He smiled faintly. "That's good of you.
But…that's the thing, see. You see all this misery
and hatred and lying. And you can't even tell anybody else about it. You have to tough it out on the
job. You can't let the other guys think you're a wuss.
You have to pretend that you can stand there and
look at a dead body and not want to…'' He broke
off and sighed. "What's really bad is after a while
you get to where you *can* look at it and not feel much

of anything. Then when you go home, it's not like telling your wife or your girlfriend about your bad day at the office or your problems with the boss. Nobody should have to listen to this kind of thing. So you keep it all inside you.''

"I would think…even if it's bad, if someone cared for you, they'd want to hear what troubled you.''

"In theory, I guess. But in reality—who can stand to hear gruesome stories or even just constant tales about avarice and greed and people's inhumanity to each other? So all you do is go to the bar after you get off shift and have a few beers with the other guys and joke around and hope that you don't turn into a bitter shell like some of the older ones.''

"Is that always what happens?"

"I don't know. It happens a lot. Cops get very cynical. You don't trust anybody. You're always looking for the lies people are telling. You could see somebody giving away money, and you'd think, 'What's his con?'"

"I can see you would."

"You start to think that everyone in the world is bad. And it seems hopeless. Like there's nothing you can do about it—it's all just going to go on and on, and what you do doesn't help a bit.''

"Is that why you quit the police force?"

"Yeah. I didn't like the person it was turning me into.'' He frowned, tired lines settling on his face in a way that made Lisa want to lean forward and smooth them away with her fingertips.

He took another swig of beer, then set the bottle

on the low table in front of the couch and sat back. He looked over at Lisa.

"I'm sorry. I didn't mean to come over here and bring you down like this. I should have stayed at home."

"No. I'm glad you came." Lisa smiled. "I like you when you're joking and having fun. But this is who you are, too. It's—I like to see the person who's inside you, the serious one. I'm glad that you're affected by things like that...and that you trust me enough to tell me."

His mouth quirked up wryly. "It's not something I normally do with attorneys."

Lisa made a face. "We aren't talking legal issues here. We're talking about emotions."

"Yeah..."

"So...did you have a wife that you couldn't tell those things to?"

"No." He paused for a moment, then added quietly, "I did have a girlfriend, the last year or so I was in San Antonio. But that was—ah, hell, she was part of the whole meltdown."

"What do you mean?"

He glanced at Lisa, then shrugged. "I met her at a bar. She was there with a bunch of people that I knew. She wasn't connected with the law, and I liked that. I'd dated some women who were cops or prosecutors." He cast her a teasing glance. "Even a defense attorney. And it's nice 'cause you know the same world, sort of, but on the other hand, you're always in that world. It's like there's nothing else out there, no normal life. You know?''

Lisa nodded.

Quinn picked up the beer and took another swallow. He began to talk, looking at the beer bottle and picking at the label. ''Her name was Jennifer. She was a smart lady, ambitious, hardworking. I guess I'm attracted to women like that. Anyway, I fell for her pretty hard.''

Lisa's stomach knotted at his words, and she realized, with some surprise that what she was feeling was jealousy—the same little itching, nasty feeling that had prompted her to ask whether he'd had a wife. Firmly she pushed the feeling away and concentrated on Quinn's words.

''She worked for a major company there, and she had risen through the ranks quickly. She was in marketing, and she worked for the vice president in charge of the department. He reported right to the CEO. So she was in a good position, young for the job, on the fast track to success.''

''You sound like that was a problem.''

''I didn't think it was. I mean, it meant I didn't get to see her as much as I'd like. She had a busy schedule, and it didn't always fit with a cop's hours. But I could live with that. I admired her for her abilities, her determination.''

''What happened?''

''My partner and I were working a case. Well, it got bigger and bigger, and pretty soon there was a whole task force of us. It started out in Robbery—

we were investigating a certain fence, and pretty soon we realized that there was a ring of them, and when we tried to trace who owned the shops, we found ourselves coming on this whole network. There were tentacles everywhere, going to prostitution, extortion, gambling. We had to bring in financial experts. They were trying to follow the paper trails, sift through the dummy corporations. It was a big operation. And the thing was, eventually, it led back to the corporation that Jennifer worked for.''

"What?" Lisa's eyes opened wide. "You mean she was involved in it?"

"No. No, nothing like that. The company she worked for was legitimate, except we had the suspicion that they might have been laundering money through it. Several of the companies were legit. But not the CEO. He was the head of the crime ring. We were sure of it. The hard part, of course, was proving it—because of the tangle of corporations.

"Well, I was torn. I couldn't tell her about our operation—I mean, we were working in the utmost secrecy by that point. We couldn't risk anything getting back to the main guy. So I kept my mouth shut. But I was worried. I hated her working for somebody like that. I was afraid she would be mad at me for not telling her and letting her continue to work for a crook. And even though what she did was legit, there was always the chance that there would be some stain attached to anybody who worked for him—if and when we caught him, of course. That was beginning to look pretty iffy. We knew he was the man, but we couldn't show a clear, direct link. Then we got a big break. We turned his accountant. He was able to link the man directly to all the crimes. We had our case. We started making arrests.''

"Was Jennifer mad at you?"

"No. She understood why I couldn't tell her. She was shocked, of course, to find out about the boss. All the people who worked for him were. She had had a fair amount of dealings with him, working as she did for the head of marketing. I figured she would quit, look for another job, but she didn't. She had a big marketing campaign going—it was her baby. She said it would fall apart if she left. Her immediate boss needed her. I understood that, and anyway, she worked for the corporation, not him. When he went to jail, I guessed the legitimate business would go on, free of him. Only he didn't go to jail. The accountant, the one who could make all the connections, mysteriously disappeared.''

"They had him killed?" Lisa asked, caught up in the story.

"I imagine. Only we couldn't find a body. It was barely possible that he had decided to split and not testify—maybe his former boss paid him a big bundle of money to disappear. But I don't think so. We were giving him immunity. If he didn't have our protection, he knew he would be in serious danger, even if they did pay him off. Death's the only way to be sure he wouldn't ever talk. Besides, he had betrayed the guy. We were sure he'd had the accountant killed. We looked for the body, but they had done a good job of covering it up. There was nothing. Our case was also nothing. We knew he did it. We had enough proof to close down a bunch of the illegal operations. But we couldn't get him. Without the accountant's testimony, we didn't have a case against him.''

"What happened?"

"He walked. We couldn't even indict him. He went back to his business. And Jennifer kept working for him. I couldn't believe it.'' His mouth twisted humorlessly as he thought back to what had happened. "I was still naive—after all that time, all the stuff I'd seen, I still was naive enough to think that she wouldn't work for him because he was crooked. I figured when he returned and she'd have to be working with him again, she would leave. But she didn't. We had a big argument about it. I wanted her to leave. I should have realized that it was pointless. What I really wanted, I guess, was for her to *want* to leave because he was crooked. For her to feel that it was the right thing to do. But she didn't. She said she was getting a promotion because her marketing campaign had done so well. She would head up a new department they were creating, and she would be reporting directly to the CEO.''

"The crook?" Lisa exclaimed.

"Yeah.'' Bitterness tinged his voice. "The crook. She was going to have a lot more money and power and prestige. It was everything she wanted. I pointed out to her that he was a criminal. She said he hadn't even been brought to trial. We didn't have proof, we just had suspicions. I told her we were certain, and I pointed out that the only reason he hadn't been brought to trial was because he had in all probability had our witness killed! She said there was no proof of that. She said that her company and what she did was legitimate, anyway. I told her we couldn't stay together if she did that. I couldn't be involved with someone who worked for a criminal. And she looked me straight in the eye and said she already knew that—he had already told her that she couldn't work for him and be involved with one of the cops who was after him.''

"Oh, Quinn…" Lisa didn't know what to say to him. What could possibly ease the hurt of such a betrayal?

"Her job was all that mattered to her, her ambition. She was willing to give me up. She was willing to work for someone without morals. She didn't care as long as she got ahead. So there I was, the case I had devoted my life to for a year went bust. The bad guy walked. And the woman I loved chose him and her career over me. That's when I quit the force and moved back to Angel Eye.''

"I'm sorry. Oh, Quinn, I'm so sorry.'' Lisa slid across the couch to him, her arms going around him instinctively. She knew now why his sister had called him 'guarded,' why he had stuck to short-term, casual relationships.

He remained stiff for a moment, then his arms clamped around her tightly, and Quinn buried his face in the crook of her neck, holding on to her as if he would never let her go.

Lisa was a little amazed at the pleasure that washed through her at simply being in Quinn's arms like this. The weight of his head against her shoulder, the warmth of his body, the hard strength of his bones and muscles against her—all filled her with a deep sense of satisfaction and peace, as if something missing for a long time was finally there, as if she *belonged* there.

He shifted, turning so that they were lying down on the couch, arms around each other, cocooned in warmth. His lips brushed her hair.

"Thank you," he murmured.

Lisa nestled into him, closing her eyes and luxuriating in the comfort and strength of lying against him. She heard his breathing slip gradually into the steady, slow rhythm of sleep. Her lips curved up into a smile. She should get up, she thought, and send him home to bed, but it was much too nice to lie here with him. She didn't know why it felt so good, so right, to feel his hard body relaxing against her, but she knew that she could not bring it to an end just yet. Lisa shifted into a more comfortable position, turning her back into him, and he adjusted in his sleep, his arm looping over her. She would just lie here for a moment longer, she thought....

She was dreaming about Quinn: a hot, sensual dream. He was naked and in a bathtub, his head leaning back against the rim, eyes closed, and steam rose all around them. She knelt beside him, her hand sliding soapily over his chest. His skin was slick beneath her fingers, hard bone padded by muscle. His face was slack with sensual pleasure, and small noises of enjoyment escaped from him as her hand roamed over his body. Her breasts felt full and heavy, and there was a growing ache between her legs, warm and insistent. She stirred, moving her legs to ease the yearning there.

Then they were on a porch, and it was she who was naked now. She knew that they should go inside, that anyone who happened by could see them there, but she could not bring herself to move. Quinn was behind her now, his quickening manhood pressing against her buttocks, his hands roaming over the front of her. His hand was at her waist, and she reached up and put her own hand over his, pushing his hand farther down, guiding it toward the blossoming ache between her legs, seeking the fulfillment that only he could bring. Then his hand was there, slipping in between her legs, pressing into her.

Pleasure rocketed through her, hot and quick, so startling that her eyes flew open, and she was jolted out of her sleep. She blinked, trying to gather her wild, scattered thoughts. Her whole body felt on fire; Quinn's body behind her was a furnace. In her sleep, her old robe had twisted around her, the belt loosening, and the two sides gaped open. Just as in her dream, her hand was on top of his, guiding his hand in between her legs, and her legs were clamped tightly around it, the hot pleasure that had brought her awake pulsing in waves through her.

She closed her eyes, her face flushing hot with embarrassment. Simply dreaming about him had brought her to climax, and she was still hot and aching for him. She could only hope that he was still asleep and did not know how she had responded to him in her sleep.

Behind her, Quinn stirred, groaning faintly. He shifted in his sleep, throwing his leg over her. She was glad that he was obviously still asleep, but the new intimacy of their position aroused her even more. She pressed her lips together, trying to will away the throbbing urgency within her. Quinn's hand slid up to her waist, pressing her more tightly against him.

"Lisa," he murmured, and the very sound of her name in his mouth stirred her. Asleep, he had said *her* name, not anyone else's, not even that of the woman he had loved in San Antonio.

She felt his whole body stiffen suddenly, and she knew that he, too, had awakened. She heard his breath, short and quick. His hand spread out over her stomach caressingly.

"Lisa," he said again, his voice a caress in itself, and nuzzled into her hair. His hand roamed over the bare skin of her stomach, moving down until it touched the elastic of her panties, then gliding back up until his knuckles brushed the underside of her breast.

He murmured something unintelligible as his lips

pressed into the skin of her neck, and he cupped her breast. Lisa could not contain a small moan of pleasure as he gently cradled her breast, his thumb circling her nipple. Her nipples prickled and hardened, shivers running out through her. A long shudder shook Quinn, and he rose up on his arm, turning her to him, his mouth seeking hers hungrily.

Lisa wrapped her arms around his neck, pressing herself against him, her mouth eagerly answering him. She wanted him deep inside her, easing the ache between her legs, filling and fulfilling her. Warm and hazy with sleep, for the moment she thought of nothing but her need, the elemental hunger inside her for him.

He took her nipple between his forefinger and thumb, tenderly squeezing and rolling it so that it hardened. His mouth left hers, trailing molten kisses down her throat and onto her chest. Pushing aside the loose folds of her robe, he exposed her breasts, and for a moment he paused, looking at the full, soft orbs, centered by pink-brown nipples, tight with desire for him.

Then he bent and brushed his lips against each nipple, with feathery kisses arousing them even more. Her breasts were heavy and aching for him, and when at last his mouth settled upon one nipple, pulling it into his mouth with a firm, wet suction, Lisa gasped at the sheer pleasure that coursed down through her, exploding like fire in her abdomen. She groaned, digging her hands into his hair and arching up.

Lisa had dated, had even been serious enough with two men that they had become lovers, but never had she felt as she did now. Never before had she felt as if her entire being was consumed with flame, as if she hungered and thirsted for a man. The touch of Quinn's calloused fingers against her skin was driving her to the brink of madness, it seemed. Each touch of his lips and flicker of his tongue increased the heated throbbing between her legs until she felt as if she would explode with a passion too great to contain. She moved restlessly beneath him, her fingers digging into his arms in a way that would have been painful had he not been too far lost in his own passion to feel it.

Quinn slid farther down, his mouth moving over the smooth skin of her stomach, his breath rasping in his throat, blood pounding in his head. He had come awake suddenly, hot and hard, pulsing with need for her. He wanted her with a desperate, primitive hunger, wanted to taste her and feel her in every way, to lose himself deep within her.

However, they were lying on a couch, and as he moved down, heedless of everything but the yearning inside him, his feet encountered the arm of the sofa, and, with an impatient twist, the large lamp that stood on the end table. The lamp turned over with a crash, rolling off the end table and thudding onto the floor, sending the room into darkness.

Quinn cursed, briefly and vividly. Lisa froze, startled into awareness of her situation. Suddenly she saw herself, wild with hunger, not the rational woman in control of herself and her life that she usually was, but a creature possessed by a passion so fiery it consumed her—wanton, even animalistic, panting and moaning with desire.

"No!" She scrambled out from beneath Quinn.

Chapter 7

Lisa moved a safe distance away from Quinn, wrapping her robe around her. She trembled, her body still pulsing with need, but her mind in control once again, astonished and embarrassed by her loss of control.

Quinn groaned and sat up, bracing his elbows on his knees and shoving his hands back into his hair. "Lisa..."

"No. I'm sorry. I don't know what—I'm usually not like this."

"Like what? Passionate?" He stood up and started toward her, his arms reaching out to her.

Lisa took several steps back. "I don't—we hardly know each other."

"I think we know what we need to," he said huskily, but he stopped a few feet from her, not wanting to send her into further flight.

"This was a mistake." Lisa belted her robe tightly, squaring her shoulders and struggling to ignore the heat surging through her. "I don't do this normally."

"Maybe this isn't a normal situation."

"I just—I don't fall into bed easily. I have to have some feeling—"

"You're trying to tell me you don't *feel* anything for me?"

"Something besides pure lust!" Lisa snapped back.

A faint smile touched his lips. "Well, at least you'll admit to that."

"Yes, I'll admit it. I've never felt like this before. I wanted you. Still want you," she added before he could protest her choice of words again. "Please, Quinn, don't make this hard for me. You know it's not that I don't feel passion for you. I do. And I like you. I feel close to you. But I'm a cautious person. I have to know that there's really something there between us—something more than just a physical attraction, however strong it may be."

"It's strong all right." Quinn sighed, swiping a hand back through his hair. "Damn!" He turned away, walking over to pick up the lamp and set it back on the end table.

A little shakily, Lisa went to the light switch and turned it on. She turned back to find Quinn close behind her. She looked up into his face, striving for a calm demeanor.

"You know, Lisa, maybe you aren't usually like this because what's between us is unusual. Maybe it's that special. Not wrong."

Looking into his eyes, Lisa could feel herself weakening. "I don't know that it's wrong. But it—it scares me a little. Yesterday was just our first date!"

Again a brief smile flickered across his lips. "I promise I won't think you're easy."

"It's not that. Well, not entirely," she admitted with a smile. "You do have a certain reputation, and I don't want to be one of your conquests."

"Darlin', I'm the one who's been conquered here."

"No. No flirting. It's time for you to go home. I need to get some sleep."

He took her chin between his forefinger and thumb, looking intently down into her eyes. "And are you going to be able to do that?"

Lisa swallowed. How could just the look in his eyes make her want to tumble into bed with him? "Eventually," she told him, striving to keep her voice even.

"I'm thinking there's no point in my even trying," he said, his thumb caressing her chin. "You know, Lisa, that's what it's supposed to be like—the fire…the hunger. Desire isn't a rational decision."

"Maybe. But I can be rational about whether I give in to it or not."

"I wouldn't count on that. One of these days, you're going to get swept away. And I intend to be there when it happens."

He bent and brushed a light kiss across her lips, then turned and strode out the door.

Lisa decided to spend the next few days clearing her mind of Quinn Sutton. It would take a while away from him to allow her to think logically and coolly about the situation. She soon found out, however, that even though he was not there, she could not keep him out of her thoughts. She cleaned her apartment and did her laundry, but no matter how busy she kept her hands, she could not stop her mind from straying to Quinn.

Quinn did not help the situation any by calling her the next afternoon to say, "Hey, darlin', got it figured out yet?"

She chuckled, sitting down on the sofa and curling her legs up under her, warmth stealing over her. "Not yet," she admitted, a little amazed at the flirtatious note that tinged her voice.

"I could come over and help you decide," he offered, the tone of his voice leaving little doubt as to exactly how he would help.

"I don't think so."

"You're a hard woman. You know, I was thinking."

"Mmm, that sounds dangerous."

"If not knowing me all that well is what's holding

you back, then the best thing to do is get to know me. Right?''

Lisa laughed again. ''I think now you're sounding like a lawyer.''

''It only makes sense,'' he said protestingly. ''So we ought to go out again. Say tomorrow night.''

''And here I was thinking just the opposite—that we ought to spend a few days without seeing each other. Give us some time to evaluate the situation.''

''The situation?'' he repeated. ''Is that what it is?''

''I don't know what it is.''

''Well, I could help you there. I know what it is.''

''And what's that?''

''I think it's called falling like a rock for somebody.''

''Or maybe it's rushing in where angels fear to tread.''

''Are we going to sit here trading clichés or are we going to have supper tomorrow night?''

''Quinn…you're impossible.''

''So I've been told.''

In the end, she wound up accepting his invitation, as she had known she would all along. They went out to dinner and a movie, and afterward they went back to her apartment for a drink and a few soul-stirring kisses. But, a little to her surprise—and, she had to admit, disappointment—he did not urge her to go further than their kisses but left before midnight, saying that he had to get up early the next morning. Lisa wandered around the apartment restlessly after his departure, unable to go to sleep, but unable to concentrate on anything like a book or even a television show. She had wanted him to stay, she knew; she had expected him to at least *try*. She could hardly fault him for being a gentleman or for giving her the space and time she had told him she needed. But it did make her feel somewhat miffed that he seemed able to leave her so easily. She could not help but wonder if he really felt the same degree of passion for her that she did for him—to her great annoyance, she could not stop thinking about what it would be like to give in and make love with Quinn. She had never experienced this sort of desire before; all the time during their date, she had had to fight back thoughts of kissing him, of sliding her hand beneath his shirt to feel the smooth flesh of his chest, of lying back on her bed and reaching up to pull him down on top of her.

When they had begun kissing, she had known that she was perilously close to letting nature take its course. And then he had pulled away, saying he had to go—and leaving her hot and dissatisfied and unsure whether she was more irritated at him or herself. Was he struggling with his passion—or did he just not care? Or was he playing some sort of game with her? He was, after all, far more experienced at this sort of thing than she.

Two days later, Quinn called and invited her to his house for supper. This, Lisa was sure, would be a seduction attempt. *A cozy dinner at his house… candlelight…music…his bed only a few tempting feet away…* The nerves in her stomach began to jump, and she wasn't sure whether it was more from anxiety or eagerness.

He offered to pick her up, but Lisa insisted on driving over herself. She was not sure how she was going to handle any attempt at seduction, but she was certain that she wanted to retain control of her ability to leave whenever she wanted. She tried on and discarded four outfits, rejecting one as too plain—this wasn't a business dinner, for heaven's sakes—and another as too alluring—she didn't want him to think she was encouraging him to seduce her, after all—and after studying them for several minutes, she began to wonder why she had bought the other two dresses at all.

Finally, annoyed with herself, she pulled on a plain pair of khaki pants and one of her favorite tops and drove over to Angel Eye, trying to quell the butterflies that were now loose inside her.

She pulled up in front of Quinn's house, faintly surprised by the small, almost quaint little house and its well-tended front yard. She got out of her car and walked up the old, cracked sidewalk to the front porch, very aware of the curtains twitching aside in the house next door and of the old man walking a little dog farther down the street who stopped in his tracks, watching with open curiosity. *Life in a small town.* She had little doubt that there were other eyes watching around the block. The thought that Quinn had probably provided his neighbors with ample topics for gossip over the years stiffened her back.

The front door opened, and Quinn stepped out,

pushing open the screen door. He had changed into jeans, and his feet were bare. A blue shirt hung casually outside his trousers, and he was in the process of rolling down his sleeves.

"Hi. Come in." He smiled at her, his eyes warming in a way that sent tendrils of heat twisting through her abdomen.

When she reached him, he kissed her chastely on the cheek, then straightened, waving a hand toward the man walking the dog. "Hey, Mr. Halbrook, how you doing?"

He stepped back to allow her to enter and followed her inside, closing the door behind him. Lisa stopped in the hallway, glancing at the front rooms opening off the hall on either side of her. She took in the oak antique furniture.

"This isn't what I expected," she admitted.

"What? You thought there'd be mirrors on the ceiling? A big round bed on a pedestal?"

She smiled wryly. "No. I'm not sure what I thought your place would look like. But I didn't figure on antiques."

He shrugged. "I don't really think of them as antiques. Sounds too effete. They're just old farm things. Homey." He nodded his head down the hall toward the large old-fashioned kitchen at the rear. "You mind coming into the kitchen? I've got to make sure nothing's burning."

"Sure." Lisa followed him down the hall, intrigued by the image of Quinn cooking. Her eyes drifted down the long, slim line of his legs, hugged by the worn, faded blue jeans, to his bare feet. She had never realized before, she thought, how sexy bare feet and jeans could look on a man.

Quinn went to the stove to check on the pots and pans. At that moment a small head stuck itself out from behind the curtains that hung across the bottom half of the kitchen window. Piercing green eyes regarded Lisa carefully, and, an instant later, the cat jumped out from behind the curtain and landed lightly on the floor. It stalked across the floor to the center of the kitchen and stood, looking up at Lisa.

The animal was the homeliest cat that Lisa had ever seen.

"Well," Lisa said, addressing the still animal, "you look like you've been in a few fights. Only thing is, I can't tell if you won or lost."

"Oh, won," Quinn said, turning around to look at the cat, then at Lisa. "Jo-Jo's about the meanest animal I know. I figure if he looks like this, the others must have all looked a lot worse."

Lisa smiled. "I wouldn't have figured you for a cat-lover, either."

"I know. My brothers are embarrassed by me," Quinn said, grinning. "But I don't know that I love cats. It's just Jo-Jo."

"Ah, I see." She addressed the cat. "Well, I have to admit you look pretty special." She bent over, holding out her hand. "Hey, Jo-Jo, would you come say hi?"

"Better watch out. Jo-Jo's—well, unpredictable.

He sank his claws into Daniel once, and he regularly chases his dog out of the yard.''

"A watch cat, huh?" Lisa said, still smiling at Jo-Jo.

Jo-Jo blinked, then trotted over to Lisa and bumped her hand with his head. She stroked his head, and his eyes slitted in pleasure, his chest starting a rumble of pleasure.

"Wow. I've never seen him do that." Quinn regarded his pet with surprise, then cast Lisa a look of awe. "I am impressed. Jo-Jo is not a pushover."

Lisa chuckled as the cat proceeded to twine around her ankles, purring. "He just has good taste."

"That's true. Would you like a beer? A glass of wine?"

"Wine would be nice."

Lisa sat down at one of the chairs around the heavy, old-fashioned table, and watched as he finished stirring a pot and replaced the lid, then went to the cabinet to take out a wineglass. "When did you get Jo-Jo?"

"I didn't, exactly. He got me. Not too long after I moved back here, one day I came home and there he was, lurking in the bushes outside. He looked like he'd been in a fight. He was pretty wary, though, wouldn't come inside or even come close to me. So I set out some food for him, and after I'd leave, he would come out and eat it. I started leaving it on the porch, and he would come up there, and finally one day he let me touch him. Then one afternoon, when I came home from work and opened the front door, he just trotted right in like he owned the place and lay down on the sofa in the living room. Been here ever since." He cast an affectionate look at the animal as he carried the glass over to Lisa. "He still sneaks out and gets into fights sometimes, though, the old reprobate."

Lisa cast him a speaking look. "I'm sure you wouldn't have it any other way."

Quinn grinned at her. "I have to admit, I always like the feisty ones." He sat down and rested his arm on the table, sliding his hand over and lightly running a finger along her arm. "I'm glad you came over tonight."

Lisa could think of nothing to say; the touch of his skin on hers took away all thought. She was aware of nothing but the faint tug of his rougher flesh against hers, the light in his mahogany eyes as they gazed into hers, the heat that surged in her at his nearness.

He curled his hand around her palm and lifted her hand, pressing his lips against her fingers. "I kept thinking about you today. Fact is, I had trouble thinking about anything else."

"Quinn…"

"I know. You're not sure." He gave her hand a squeeze and let it go, standing up. "I'm not pushing, just stating a fact." He moved toward the stove, saying over his shoulder, "Now, how do you feel about chicken cacciatore?"

"If that's what's making that delicious odor I've been smelling, then I think I feel very good about it,'' Lisa joked, folding her hands together to hide the faint trembling in them.

They kept the conversation on a light plane all through dinner, and afterward they sat in the swing on the front porch, desultorily talking and enjoying the pleasant October air. Quinn looped his arm around her shoulders, but the curiosity of his neighbors made his front porch too public a place for anything more.

''I have the feeling that everyone on the block is watching us,'' Lisa joked.

Quinn let out a little grunt. ''You wouldn't be far wrong.''

''Is everyone in a small town like this?''

''They're interested,'' he replied.

''How do you stand it?''

He shrugged. ''Well, the reason they're so curious is because they care. Because they know you. In the city, you see two people together, and they're total strangers to you. What do you care about them? Here, people know you. You're one of their own. So they're interested in what you're doing. Now, they're probably more interested in what's going on here because I'm the sheriff. So everybody kind of feels like they have a say in what I do. Mr. Miller, across the street there, couldn't care less what I do. He likes to sit in the dark every night and watch TV. But Mrs. Knight, next door, thinks she's my substitute mother. She brings me cookies and cakes and things, so she'll want to know whether you're good enough for me.''

''Well, I like that!''

He chuckled. "But Aaron Halbrook, the guy who was walking his dog, is only interested in whether I catch the graffiti artists."

"Graffiti artists? Where is there graffiti?"

"Water tower west of town is the favorite place. Every year or two, some kid who's graduating from high school that year likes to climb the water tower and paint 'Seniors' and his class's year on it. There's also a big rock on the highway north of here that's a pretty good spot, too. We drive extra patrols past them around graduation time."

"And is that the height of crime in Angel Eye?"

"According to Aaron, it is. He also plays poker with my dad, so that gives him extra authority to complain, you see."

"Of course."

"Mrs. Pena, next to Mr. Miller on your right, is part of the very large and interconnected family network of my night dispatcher, Lena. You met her at the wedding."

"Yeah, I remember. She and Rita Delgado invited me to make tamales at Christmas."

"Right. Well, Mrs. Pena's house is dark so that we can't see her standing at her front window watching. Quite frankly, it wouldn't surprise me if she's using binoculars. Probably has a portable phone in her hand, reporting to Lena."

Lisa laughed.

"I'm serious. It's a point of honor with her. She would be mortified if she wasn't the first on the phone to Lena with any news about me. 'Course, it wouldn't be as bad if I weren't single.''

"Mmm, I can see that you wouldn't provide as much entertainment."

"Now, there you go again, assuming I'm a swinging bachelor. I don't know whether I should be flattered you think I have so much appeal or appalled at your opinion of my morals."

"Well, you know…I heard that you date a lot."

He looked at her evenly. "That doesn't mean I sleep with them all."

Lisa gazed back at him, surprised and pleased by his words. "Really?"

"Yeah, really." He paused, then said. "In fact, the reason they're so all-fired curious about you is because they never see a woman over here."

"You're kidding. Why not?"

"It's usually not worth stirring up the gossip. So they know that you're special."

Lisa's breath caught in her throat. Her heart was suddenly pounding, and she was aware of a strong urge to throw herself into his arms. How could such simple words have the power to affect her so much?

He grinned. "Well, now I know how to shut you up." He rose, extending his hand down to her. "Come on, you probably better get on home now, or my neighbors will all lose too much sleep."

Lisa took his hand and stood up. She found herself reluctant to go. *Was he not even going to kiss her?*

"You'll need your purse, right?" He led her inside and closed the door behind them.

Then he turned, his eyes alight, his hands going to her waist, and he backed her up against the door to give her a long, thorough kiss. When finally he raised his head, he smiled, saying, "Handy things, purses."

Lisa chuckled, stretching up on tiptoe to kiss him again.

After several minutes, Quinn pulled back reluctantly. "Unfortunately, purses aren't a very time-consuming excuse." He kissed her gently on each eyebrow, then the tip of her nose. "I don't want you to leave."

"I don't want to, either," Lisa admitted honestly.

The heat in his eyes went up a notch, and he pulled her back against him. "Maybe we'll just let them talk."

His hand moved down her back, pressing her firmly against his taut body. Reluctantly Lisa shook her head. "No. We better not."

She looked up into his face, and she knew that he could see in hers that she was fast running out of resistance. He bent and kissed her lips gently.

"Next time," he said, his voice rife with promise.

Lisa was sitting at her desk the next morning, papers spread in front of her, dreamily thinking about the evening before, when the shrill buzz of the phone broke her reverie.

"Benny Hernandez, line one," Kiki announced.

Lisa pushed in the button for the line. "Lisa Mendoza."

"Miss Mendoza!" Benny's voice was thin and jumpy.

"Yes? Is something the matter?"

"He picked me up again. They've got me down at the sheriff's office."

"Qui—Sheriff Sutton arrested you?"

"No. Two deputies came out to the house and picked me up, said he wanted to talk to me. They brought me down here, and I said I had to talk to you."

"You did the right thing, Benny. I'll be right over. Don't say anything until I'm with you. Do you know what they want to talk to you about?"

"I—I think it's something about that dead guy." Fear tinged Benny's words.

"I'll be there as soon as I can."

Lisa hung up the phone. She felt blindsided. Quinn had said nothing about intending to haul her client in for questioning today. She was sure he had known what he was going to do. It was nine o'clock in the morning; his deputies had obviously gone to Benny's first thing today.

Setting her jaw, she picked up the jacket to her suit and put it on, grabbed her briefcase and purse and headed out the door. "I'm going to the county courthouse," she told Kiki grimly on her way out.

Anger and hurt sped her on her way to Angel Eye. Quinn had intentionally not told her about this; he wanted to spring it on Benny, probably hoping that Benny would not have the presence of mind to ask for his attorney. Of course, Quinn had no obligation to tell her, but still, she could not help but feel as if she had been tricked. He was playing cop games, she thought, and that thought led inevitably to the question of what other games he was playing.

However, she knew that she could not afford to let personal feelings enter into the interview before her. She was Benny's attorney; she had to represent him to the best of her ability, and that meant not letting her personal feelings interfere. She must be cool and calm and logical. If she let emotions into this, she would be giving Quinn an advantage.

By the time she reached the county courthouse, she had talked herself into at least the appearance of a businesslike calm. She strode into the courthouse and down the hall to the sheriff's office. A deputy jumped up from his desk when she entered and escorted her down the hall to a small windowless room where Quinn and her client sat across a small table from each other. Quinn was steadily watching Benny. Benny had his eyes turned down to his hands, clenched tightly together in his lap.

"Hello, Benny," Lisa said, adding with a polite nod, "Sheriff."

"Ms. Mendoza." Quinn rose to his feet, unsmiling, but there was an unmistakable warmth to his eyes.

Lisa shifted her gaze away from him and sat down beside her client. "All right, Sheriff, what is this about?"

"I had a few questions I wanted to ask Benny."

"What questions?"

"I think he can help me identify a body."

Quinn reached over to a manila file folder on the table beside him and flipped it open. He took out a black-and-white picture from the file and slid it casually across the table to Benny.

"You know this man, Benny?"

Benny's eyes went down to the photo, and he paled. Lisa, looking over at the photograph, saw that it showed a corpse on a metal table, a sheet covering it below the shoulders. Benny shook his head rapidly. "No. I don't know him. Who is this guy?"

"Look carefully, Benny." Quinn flopped down another photo, this one closer to the corpse's face. It was coldly gruesome, and Lisa swallowed back bile.

"What is the purpose of this, Sheriff?" she asked with more poise than she felt. "My client has already told you that he does not recognize the man. May we leave now?"

Quinn ignored her words, pulling out another picture and showing it to Benny. This time it was of the same corpse, clothed and lying in a field. It was, if anything, even worse.

"No, man!" Benny said faintly, his skin taking on a sallow, almost green tint. "I never seen him before."

"Are you sure?" Quinn did not remove the pictures. Benny kept his eyes carefully turned toward the table beside them. "We found this guy in a field last weekend. I think he may have something to do with your friends."

"I don't know what you're talking about."

"I think you do. This man had no identification on him. Obviously Hispanic. I'm thinking he's an illegal alien."

"So?" Benny asked, crossing his arms across his chest and turning his eyes back to Quinn defiantly.

"So I'm thinking he's one of the illegals that you and your friends have been bringing into the country. Maybe even one you brought in yourself."

Benny said nothing. After a moment, Quinn went on, "What do you do over in old man Rodriguez's house? Do you put the illegals up there for a while, or do you just switch drivers there? You know, at first I figured it for a car-theft ring, but it's a lot more than that, isn't it? You guys aren't chopping cars. You're trafficking in human beings."

Benny's nostrils flared, and he opened his mouth.

Lisa quickly interjected, "You don't need to answer him, Benny." She turned toward Quinn. "My client has answered your questions. He cannot identify these pictures. You have no further reason to hold him or question him."

"Oh, I think I do." Quinn kept his eyes on Benny as he spoke, flat and cold. He seemed an entirely different person from the man Lisa knew, and she found it chilling. "Benny knows what I'm talking about, don't you, Ben? You quit your job several months ago, but somehow or other, you've got more money than you did back when you were working. You're buying clothes, stereo equipment. That's what your grandmother tells me. She's worried about you, son. She's afraid you're going to follow in your father's footsteps and wind up in Huntsville.''

''He's not my father!''

''No, that's right. He's your stepfather. But you're looking a lot like him right now.''

Benny's lips curved in a sneer. Lisa was poised, ready to jump in if he started to speak, but he kept quiet.

''You've always been a pretty good kid, Benny,'' Quinn said now, his voice softening. ''A few minor scrapes—lots of kids get into a little trouble like that. But smuggling in illegal aliens, that's not a little scrape. That's big.'' He paused for a moment. ''Maybe you think you're doing a good thing, helping out some poor people who just want a chance to work and live in this country. But it didn't turn out too good for this guy, did it?''

His tone hardened and he tapped the photo in front of Benny. ''It turns out like this for lots of them. Do you have any idea how many people die in the desert after they cross the border? Abandoned by the people they trusted to guide them? Or stuffed into a closed, broiling-hot truck in the summer?''

He was quiet for a moment, letting his words hang in the air. Benny had turned his gaze back to his hands again, his jaw set. Quinn went on, ''What happens to them after you bring them to the old man's house? Where do they go from there? Do you take them on or does somebody else do that? They just turning them loose in San Antonio or Austin? Or do they take them on, to work camps? Do you know about those? Have you seen them?''

''I don't know what you're talking about,'' Benny said sullenly, glancing up at Quinn.

''No, you probably don't. They wouldn't show them to you. They wouldn't want you to know what happens to some of those guys you bring in. They wouldn't want you to see the prisons where they stick them. That's what they are, Benny. These people are looking for freedom, and what they get is stuck in a shack with no running water and a big locked fence all around the place to make sure they don't get out at night. Concertina wire all along the top. They come in trucks in the morning to load them up and take them to their jobs. Working in some field all day in the hot sun. Or maybe stuck in a cramped, airless little factory turning out clothes. Then when it gets dark, they load them back up and take 'em out to the camp again, where they get a meal you'd turn your nose up at. Then they can go to sleep on a little cotton mattress on the floor—if the insects and rats let them, of course.''

''Sheriff Sutton!'' Lisa snapped. ''What is the purpose of all this?''

Quinn glanced at her and back to Benny. ''I just thought Benny might like to know what happens to some illegals after they get brought into the country. It's real damn easy to take advantage of people who are scared to go to the law, who don't speak the language, who don't want to be caught and sent back home.''

"It's very sad," Lisa agreed in a clipped voice, "but it has nothing to do with my client."

"Is that right, Benny?" Quinn drawled. "You got nothing to do with illegal aliens?"

"No!" Benny snapped. "I told you. I don't know what you're talking about."

"I think you do. But there's more to it than that. It's not just a question of smuggling in illegals. This man in the pictures…" Quinn tapped the photos again, his eyes boring into Benny's. "He died of cocaine poisoning. There was a condom full of it in his colon, and it ruptured, started leaking. He wasn't only an illegal, he was a mule. He was smuggling in drugs."

Chapter 8

Benny's eyes widened, and he pulled back in his chair. "You're lying!"

"No, I'm not," Quinn replied quietly. "You've gotten yourself involved in smuggling drugs."

"No!" Benny shook his head. "I don't know anything about that. I'm not smuggling nothing!"

"How would you know if the people you're driving are carrying the drugs inside them?" Quinn pointed out reasonably.

"I'm not driving them! I don't know what you're talking about," Benny said stubbornly. "And I don't know that guy." He shoved the pictures back across the table toward Quinn. "Leave me alone."

"Sheriff, my client has answered all your questions," Lisa said firmly. "Unless you intend to charge Mr. Hernandez, it's time that you released him.''

Quinn looked at her. ''No. I don't plan to charge him with anything…yet.'' He stood up, shoving back his chair, and his voice was charged with irritation. ''Okay, Benny, you're a real smart guy. You've got your lawyer. You're going to stonewall it all the way to prison. You're going to go down for your buddies. What do you care about these people dying? What do you care about the drugs they're bringing in? You're a tough guy.''

He walked over and opened the door to the interview room, jerking his head toward the open doorway. ''Go on. Get out.''

Benny stood, jamming his hands in his pockets, and walked out the door, his head down. Lisa followed him, not looking at Quinn. She caught up with Benny as he pushed through the front door of the courthouse and started down the steps.

''Benny, wait!''

He stopped and turned. His face was pale, and his eyes big and dark in it. He looked very young and almost on the brink of tears.

''I didn't know that guy, Ms. Mendoza. I swear I've never seen him before in my life! You have to believe me.''

''I do.''

''He doesn't.'' He glanced toward the building.

''The sheriff was fishing, Benny,'' Lisa said confidently. ''Trying to rattle you into saying something.''

"But I couldn't! I didn't know him. I didn't," he repeated, as if it were a mantra. His face twisted. "God, I've never seen anything like that."

"It was gruesome. More cop tricks."

"Yeah, I know." Benny still looked queasy.

"Do you need a ride home?"

"Nah. I think I'll walk."

Lisa nodded. Benny looked as though he could use some time alone. Besides, she had a few things she wanted to say to the sheriff.

She watched Benny walk down the steps, then she turned and marched back into the courthouse and through the hall to the sheriff's office. She walked straight into Quinn's private office and closed the door behind her. He stood up as she entered and came around the desk toward her.

"Hey, darlin'."

"Don't you 'hey, darlin'' me," Lisa retorted. "You knew about this last night, didn't you? And you didn't say a word to me!"

"Yeah, I knew." He stopped, looking a little wary.

"Why didn't you tell me you were going to haul Benny in here this morning? What kind of game are you playing with me? Is romancing the defense attorney one of your ploys for getting information?"

"No!" Quinn's brows rushed together. "How can you say that? I'm not playing any kind of game with you. Damn it, Lisa, I was trying to keep our personal and business lives separate. I wouldn't have called up any other lawyer and said, 'Hey, listen, I'm bringing in your client for questioning tomorrow, so get prepared for it.' I couldn't very well tell *you*. I can't play favorites, Lisa.''

"I'm not asking you to play favorites!" Lisa crossed her arms and turned away, walking over to the window to look out. She knew Quinn was right. He had treated her as he would have treated any other attorney, as far as bringing Benny in for questioning went. What she was feeling, she realized, was hurt because he *hadn't* treated her specially because of his affection for her. She was reacting like a girlfriend, not a lawyer.

"I'm sorry," she said stiffly, continuing to look out the window instead of at him. "You're right. You were acting professionally. I was not."

"You weren't unprofessional."

"No." Lisa turned back to face him squarely. "I was. I wanted you to give me special treatment."

"It's only natural—"

"Yes, it probably is. But that's exactly the reason why it's a bad idea to mix our professional and personal lives." Lisa was swamped with a wave of sadness. "I should never have done this."

"Wait. What are you talking about? You should never have done what?"

"Gotten involved with you. It's all wrong. I've let my personal feelings get all mixed up with my job. It's not fair to my client. It's not fair to you."

"Honey, it's not that bad." Quinn went to her, reached out to pull her into his arms comfortingly.

"No." Lisa twisted away. "You wouldn't be putting your arms around some other attorney because he felt bad.''

Quinn chuckled. ''No. I've never been attracted to those guys, frankly.''

''I'm serious. It's unfair. It makes all our dealings about my client questionable. *Are you going easy on me? Am I favoring you?*'' She looked back at Quinn, and it felt as if a knife were being twisted in her chest. ''It's not feasible. I can't go on seeing you.''

''What?'' Quinn looked stunned. ''Because of this one thing?''

''It's not just this one thing. Benny is obviously a suspect in your case. I don't know how far you intend to go with it. For all I know, it could end up in a trial. I cannot allow the case to be tainted because I was dating the sheriff!''

''No. Lisa, come on. We can deal with it. We can work something out. You're not used to separating your work from your feelings. It took you by surprise. But with a little practice—''

''I don't want to have to separate my work from my feelings,'' Lisa retorted. ''I am very involved with what I do. I bring my emotions to it. How can I effectively defend my client when I—when I care for you? You are the enemy at that moment, and I have trouble seeing you as that.''

''You are not going to shortchange Benny because you like me,'' Quinn said. ''You're too good a lawyer for that.''

''It works the other way, too, you know. Today, in that room, when I looked at you, and your eyes were so hard and flat—it scared me. It was as if you were another person. I didn't like that. I don't want to feel that way." She shook her head. "I was wrong to go out with you. I—we—I have to stop seeing you."

There was a moment of shocked silence. Then Quinn said softly, "Lisa, no, there's got to be some other way."

"What?"

"It's just one case. If you feel that there's too much conflict of interest, then you can resign as his attorney. Turn the case over to someone else."

"Oh, I see," Lisa flared, anger sparking in her and wiping out the pain in her chest. "I'm supposed to give up my job now? Anytime I have a client whose interests come into conflict with your job, I should just drop my client?"

"That's not what I said," Quinn replied, irritated. "I'm talking about one case. You aren't willing to step aside on one case? I thought there was something special between us. You aren't willing to give up one client for what we have?"

"Let me ask you this," Lisa retorted. "Are you willing to jettison this case? Are you willing to give up your job for me?"

"It's not the same. Lisa, be reasonable."

"No, *you* be reasonable," Lisa shot back heatedly. "This was all a mistake. Goodbye, Quinn."

"Lisa!" He started toward her, but she hurried out the door, leaving him behind her.

* * *

She had been a fool, Lisa told herself harshly. She had known it was a mistake to get involved with Quinn, but she had been too attracted to him to listen to reason. The last thing she had needed was a relationship, especially with the sheriff of the county.

Ahead of her she saw the Moonstone Café, and, on impulse, she turned into it. She could get something to eat and take a few minutes to calm down. Surprisingly, there were only three cars parked in front, so it was also possible that Elizabeth Morgan might be free to sit down and talk. Lisa had liked her, and the thought of talking to a fellow transplant from Dallas was appealing.

She parked and walked up to the front door, then stopped when she saw the Closed sign on the door. Below it, a square sign listing the hours for the restaurant confirmed that it was closed on Mondays. Lisa sighed, disappointed, and turned back toward her car.

Before she reached it, the front door of the café opened behind her, and someone called, ''Lisa!''

She turned to see Elizabeth standing in the doorway, dressed in slacks and a blue T-shirt, her dark, curling hair piled up in a casual knot atop her head.

''You want some dinner? Come on in.''

Lisa turned and walked back to her. ''I'm sorry. I don't want to put you out. I didn't realize you were closed on Mondays.''

''Yeah, it's my day off. I have some friends that

usually come over and we have supper and talk. Why don't you join us?''

"Oh, no, I couldn't...''

"Sure. It's no problem. It's just us girls. Eve and Meredith would love to meet you.'' When Lisa hesitated, she went on in the tone of one offering a temptation, "I made lasagna....''

"Mmm.'' Lisa smiled. "That settles it. I can't resist.''

She followed Elizabeth into the café. It looked a little strange, empty like this. Two women were seated at a table that lay close to the bar and to the kitchen, and they turned toward Elizabeth and Lisa as they approached.

"Ladies, I'd like to introduce you to Lisa Mendoza,'' Elizabeth told the women. "Lisa, this is Meredith Kramer, and the redhead over there is Eve Gallagher.''

The two women greeted her in a friendly way, and Elizabeth motioned her toward the fourth seat. "What would you like to drink? I'm having beer. Meredith's got hard lemonade. And I have soft drinks and such.''

"Hard lemonade sounds nice.''

"Coming right up.'

Elizabeth moved off toward the small bar, and Lisa sat down in the chair that she had indicated. She smiled at the other two women, who were looking at her with frank interest.

"Hi. I'm sorry to intrude.''

"Heavens, no,'' Meredith said in a soft voice,

smiling. "It's just a girls' night out. It's nice to have more 'girls.'"

"True," Eve put in. "Besides, we've been dying to meet you."

"Eve..." Meredith said in an admonishing tone.

"What?" Eve gave her friend an overly innocent look. "It's the truth, isn't it?"

"You might at least let the poor woman catch her breath before you start an inquisition."

"Inquisition!" Eve's look of outrage was as comical as her expression of innocence had been. "Well, I like that! Show a little friendly interest in a newcomer, and you call it an inquisition." She swiveled toward Lisa, saying, "But now that Meredith mentions it, we want to hear all about you. And don't leave out the part about the sheriff."

"The sheriff?" Lisa could feel the blush rising in her cheeks.

"Eve, behave." Meredith, too, turned toward Lisa. "Don't pay any attention to her. If I didn't know her mother, I would say she wasn't raised right. But since I do know Mrs. Gallagher, I know it's that Eve didn't listen."

Eve chuckled. "I'm sorry, Lisa. I shouldn't put you on the spot. We'll get to know you first...*then* we'll pepper you with questions about Quinn."

"You know Sheriff Sutton?" Lisa could not keep from asking.

She also could not keep from thinking that the odds were that Eve Gallagher was someone Quinn had probably dated. She was a slender, attractive woman with short red hair and bright green eyes. She had a wide smile, and there was a twinkle in her eyes that hinted at mischief. She was dressed in jeans and a tailored blue blouse, with battered cowboy boots on her feet. With her looks and personality, Lisa could well imagine Quinn being attracted to her. From her own experience she knew full well exactly how appealing Quinn was, so it would not be at all unlikely, given the size of population in Angel Eye, that the two of them would at least have gone out, if not more.

"Oh, sure," Eve agreed readily. "I went to school with him. He was three years ahead of me, though, so he never paid me much attention." She added with a smile, "We never dated, though, if that's what you're wondering. Two redheads—can't see that working."

She leaned forward with an engaging grin. "Tell you what, we'll tell you everything we know about Quinn if you'll tell us what you know."

"Ignore her," Elizabeth said, returning with Lisa's drink. She put it down on the table in front of Lisa and sat down.

"Well, I like that." Eve made a face.

"Have you lived here all your life?" Lisa asked in some amazement. "Both of you?"

Eve let out a whoop of laughter. "Yeah. Hard to believe, isn't it?"

"I'm sorry," Lisa said quickly, embarrassed. "I didn't mean that the way it sounded."

"Sure, you did. And it's understandable," Eve replied. "My whole life all I ever wanted was to get away from Angel Eye. I left after high school, swearing never to return." She shrugged, giving a wry grin. "But here I am, back again."

"You could hardly have done anything else," Meredith told her. "Your mother needed your help."

Lisa turned toward the other woman. Meredith looked the polar opposite of her friend. She was dressed in a skirt, jacket and blouse, all in tones of beige and still crisp in appearance even though it was the end of the day. Her smooth shoulder-length bob was dark blond, parted on one side, and her eyes were a quiet gray.

"That's true," Elizabeth agreed.

"My father has Alzheimer's," Eve explained to Lisa. "It got too much for Mom to handle all by herself—she needed someone to take over the business. Gallagher Realty." She gestured toward her booted feet. I was out showing some land today. I don't usually dress like such a cowgirl."

"I'm sorry about your father," Lisa offered inadequately.

"It happens, unfortunately. Mom's the one who has really had it tough." She turned the subject back to Lisa's original question. "So I had to come back here. But Meredith, now, likes it in Angel Eye. She chose to stay here."

"It's home," Meredith said simply. She grinned at her friend. "Not everyone has a roaming spirit."

"And Elizabeth," Eve went on merrily, "actually moved here of her own free will."

Elizabeth smiled. "I like small towns. My stress level went down about seventy per cent."

"Well, we were certainly all thrilled that you moved here," Meredith assured her.

"That's true," Eve agreed readily. "You definitely raised the quality of dining in Angel Eye."

"That doesn't even begin to describe it," Meredith added. "Before the Moonstone, there wasn't much here but the Dairy Queen and Rosie's Tacos on Fourth Street."

"It was a dining wasteland," Elizabeth agreed. "That's one reason why I chose it."

"What about you, Lisa?" Eve asked. "What brought you to Angel Eye?"

"Well, actually I live in Hammond. But I came here because of a grant I got in law school." She explained the grant and its conditions and her surprise at landing in a little town.

Eve opened another beer for herself and plopped a second drink down in front of Lisa. "Okay. Now back to the original topic of conversation—Quinn Sutton."

Meredith groaned, shaking her head in despair. "Eve…"

"What? There's nothing to do in Angel Eye except gossip. Don't tell me you don't want to know how serious it is with the sheriff and Lisa. He's been the town's number-one bachelor for four years now." She turned to Lisa and asked, "Am I embarrassing you?"

Lisa smiled. "A little."

"Well, hell, a little is okay, isn't it? I'll tell you something totally embarrassing about me if you want."

Lisa had to chuckle.

"That's hardly fair," Elizabeth pointed out. "Nothing embarrasses you."

"Not true! I was embarrassed that time at Melanie Sampson's wedding when Jack Weatherby whispered a joke to me, and I started giggling and couldn't stop."

"Oh, Lord," Meredith agreed, beginning to giggle. "That *was* awful. And you snorted."

"I can't help it!" Eve cried. "I snort when I laugh. It wasn't even that funny. It was the fact that I was trying so hard *not* to laugh, and it just made me laugh all the more. Melanie still pretends it didn't happen."

Lisa laughed along with the others. She hadn't realized until just now how long it had been since she had sat around with a bunch of women friends, talking and laughing—and how much she had missed it. She also could not help thinking how much she wanted to pump the other women for information about Quinn. She realized that there was no reason to find out about Quinn—after all, only a short time before in his office she had said that she could not date him anymore. It was foolish and contradictory to be so eager to hear everything she could about him. But she pushed the thought aside—after all, what harm could it do to find out a little more about him?

"I don't mind telling you about Quinn and me,"

she began. "But there's nothing much to tell. We've only been out a few times."

"Ah…" Eve nodded, looking wise. "But Rita Delgado told me that he took you with him to his brother's wedding. That sounds pretty serious to me."

"It was our first date!" Lisa protested. "I told him I shouldn't go, but he talked me into it."

"That sounds like Quinn," Meredith said dryly.

"Well, Janice Padilla's husband is one of his deputies, and she told me that Ruben said Quinn was pretty gone over you."

Lisa told herself it was silly to feel so warmed by what Eve said, but she could not help it. "I like Quinn," she admitted, unaware of how much the smile on her face gave away. "But it's not serious. It couldn't be. We're very different—pretty much on opposite sides. And he makes me so mad sometimes that I could just scream. We fight practically every time I see him."

"Fighting can be fun," Eve stuck in with with a wicked smile. "Especially when it comes time to make up."

Lisa shook her head. "Anyway, what's the point? I'm going back to Dallas when my year here is up. And everyone's told me what a flirt he is."

"He *is* a charmer," Meredith agreed, "but I don't think he's just a flirt. I mean, given the opportunities he has…"

"True," Eve agreed. "Most of the single women in this county have been after him."

"Probably half the married ones, too," Elizabeth added.

"I remember in high school, he had a pretty long-term relationship with one girl," Eve said.

"Really? Who?" Meredith asked.

"Susan Weatherby, Jack's sister. She went off to college, and I think she wound up marrying somebody in Colorado."

"What was he like in high school?" Lisa asked.

"A hell-raiser, mostly. It's funny that he wound up being sheriff," Eve told her. "'Cause he was always getting into trouble when he was a teenager. I remember one time he and Jack and a couple of other boys got picked up by the old sheriff. I don't remember what they were doing. But their dads had to come down and bail them out. Jack's dad was mad as a hornet, and I'm sure Mr. Sutton was, too. I never would have figured Quinn would become a policeman."

"It probably made him more sympathetic," Meredith suggested. "I mean, the kids like him pretty well." She turned to Lisa, explaining, "I teach school. And most of my students think he's an okay guy. He doesn't let them get out of line—he's tough on them if they're drinking and driving. But he doesn't harass them, either."

At that moment, a buzzer sounded loudly in the kitchen, and Elizabeth jumped to her feet. "That's the lasagna."

She went into the kitchen to get the food, and Eve and Meredith began to set the table. Lisa joined them in the task, and the subject of the sheriff was dropped.

The lasagna was, as expected, delicious, and the women devoted the next few minutes to diligently eating. After that, their conversation veered off into more general topics: movies, books, clothing styles. Eve made a date with Lisa to go shopping in San Antonio the following Saturday, and all three of the others urged her to come back to their weekly get-together the following Monday. Finally, with sighs and groans, they agreed that all of them had to work the next morning and it was time to call it a night. It didn't take long for the four of them to wash the dishes they'd used and tidy up the place, and soon after, Lisa was on the road back to Hammond.

She hummed as she drove, feeling content and even optimistic. It would be so much more pleasant living here now that she had made some friends. She told herself that having friends would make it easier not to see Quinn. Pain pierced her chest at that thought, surprising in its intensity. She hadn't known the man long, she told herself. How could it hurt this much to think of not seeing him again?

She thought of his smile—the twinkle in his eyes and the way they crinkled up at the corners…the unexpected dimple that popped into his cheek… Lisa realized that she was smiling dreamily into nothing just thinking about him, and she knew that the last thing she wanted was not to date Quinn Sutton again. On the other hand, she also knew that he was the worst man she could get involved with: he was infuriating; he was investigating her client; and any involvement with him was an entanglement she did not need when she was going to be going back to Dallas in less than a year.

By the time she turned onto her street in Hammond, she was in almost as much turmoil as she had been when she had left the sheriff's office several hours earlier. She pulled into the parking lot of her apartment building and parked her car. As she got out of her car and started toward her apartment, she saw, with a curious blend of dismay and excitement, that there was a sheriff's car parked a few cars over, and Quinn Sutton was leaning against it, waiting for her.

He straightened and started toward her. His face was tight and his eyes fiery.

"Where the hell have you been?" he snapped.

Chapter 9

Lisa's eyebrows went up at his peremptory statement. "Excuse me?"

"I've been waiting for you for hours. I was about ready to send out an APB."

"I wasn't aware that I had to account to you for my whereabouts," Lisa retorted heatedly. "What are you doing here?"

"I came because I wanted to talk to you! I wanted to apologize!" He realized the incongruity of his words and his tone, and he grinned a little sheepishly. "Ah, hell…I'm sorry. You're right." He blew out a long breath. "I had no right to jump on you like that. I was just worried about you. I sat around my office for a while and then I decided to drive over here and talk to you. I couldn't imagine where you'd gone or what could be taking you so long. I was beginning to get scared that something had happened to you.''

"I stopped by the Moonstone to see Elizabeth."

"Oh, yeah. It's Monday. I should have thought of that.''

Lisa looked at him quizzically. "You know about their get-togethers? Does everyone know everything about everybody else around here?''

He shrugged. "Well, it's sort of my job to keep an eye on things. Besides, it's pretty easy—the Moonstone's closed every Monday, and Eve's and Meredith's cars are there every Monday. If I'd looked as I drove past, I would have seen your car. But I had my mind on other things.''

He paused, then said, "So what about it? Can I come inside and talk? Make my apology?''

Lisa had to smile. "Sure. I always like an apology.'' She turned and started toward her apartment, swiveling back to say in an admonitory tone, "But that doesn't mean that I've changed my mind.''

"Of course." He widened his eyes in an innocent way.

Lisa led him into her apartment, switching on the lights as she went inside. She walked to the center of the living room and turned to face him, crossing her arms over her chest. "All right.''

"All right." He cleared his throat. "Okay, well, what I wanted to say was…I was wrong to expect you to remove yourself from a case because I'm involved in it. I just saw the quickest solution to the problem, and I jumped on it. Obviously it wouldn't be fair to ask you to quit being a defense lawyer for my sake—or even that you should not take a case if it involves the sheriff's department.''

He stopped and looked at her, then added, ''But that doesn't mean that I think there's nothing we can do about it. I know we can work it out. It doesn't have to mean that we can't have a relationship.''

''I don't see how.''

''I won't accept that.'' He came closer to her. ''I don't want not to see you again, Lisa. I like you. I more than like you. You know that. I—when you're not around, I can't stop thinking about you. I keep trying to figure out how I could arrange to run into you. The other night, when I came over late and we talked—I found myself telling you things I've never said to anybody else. I'm not just somebody trying to talk you into bed with me. I want to be with you…for a long time.''

Lisa felt herself swaying toward him, drawn by the hunger and intensity of his voice. ''I want to be with you, too,'' she admitted softly. ''But how? I can't give up my clients.''

''You don't have to,'' Quinn said persuasively, reaching out and taking her hands, holding them between both of his. ''The situation isn't as bad as you think. This case—we're both already involved. But in the future—well, first of all, my department won't be involved in most of your cases. I mean, not every criminal is your client, and most of the ones you do get were arrested by the Hammond P.D. Right?''

''Yes. But there will be some who are arrested by

your office." Lisa pulled her hands away from his and backed up a step. She could not let herself be swayed by Quinn's seductive presence. She had to keep a clear head.

"In the future, when you're the defense attorney, I'll make sure that I let one of my deputies take over the case. That's usually the way it works, anyhow. I oversee them, but Ruben or one of the others is in charge of the investigation. If you're not personally dealing with me on the case, then you won't really have a conflict of interest, will you? I'll agree not to try to influence you, and you can agree not to try to influence me."

Lisa looked at him, trying to decide if she was finding his words reasonable only because she wanted so much for him to be right. "But what about now? What about Benny? I can't forsake him just because I'm attracted to you!"

"You don't have to forsake Benny. Look, I agree it's awkward. But, you know, I'm not after Benny, whatever you may think. I want to help him as much as you do. I think he's an okay kid who's gotten himself into a bad situation. I don't think he killed that guy— I believed him when he said that he'd never seen him before. But I do think he's involved with some hard-core bad guys. I don't want to see him go down with them. I don't want to see him get hurt because he's not tough enough for the rest of them. I don't want him to turn into what they are. I don't think you want any of those things for him, either. Do you?"

"No, of course not. But that doesn't mean I'm going to stand by and let you bully and harass him, either!" Lisa shot back.

Quinn half smiled. "I'm well aware of that. I'm glad the kid has you for a lawyer. I think you'll have his best interests at heart, unlike some other attorneys his bosses might hire. When it all goes down, I'd like to think that he will be getting the best advice for *him,* not the best for some drug lord."

"He will."

"I'm glad. I'd like to keep Benny out of prison."

"Then we're in agreement."

"That's what I'm saying. I promise I'm not going to try to seduce you into doing something to help me with Benny, and I can keep my head on straight enough that I'm not going to undermine my case because of the way I feel about you. Can't you say the same?"

"Yes. Of course."

"Then what's keeping us apart?" He moved toward her again, his hands reaching out to curl around her arms, his voice low and husky as he continued, "Just pride? Or fear? The sheer, stubborn unwillingness to give in?"

He was only inches away from her, his face turned down to hers. She could feel his breath, soft and warm on her cheek.

"I—I'm not sure," she murmured.

"Whatever it is, it shouldn't be," he whispered, brushing his lips against her cheek, then her mouth.

"The way I feel about you, there shouldn't be anything between us."

Again his lips touched hers, warm and velvety. Lisa could not suppress a shiver. Her whole body was taut with anticipation. She had been waiting for this moment from the first time she met Quinn. It was, she realized, inevitable. However much she might protest or avoid it, she knew now that she was only delaying what was going to happen. It didn't matter that she had known him for only a matter of weeks. It was only in her head that she didn't know him well. She knew him in a much more primitive way—in her heart, her soul, her body.

Quinn was irritating, infuriating, not at all the man she would have chosen, and she could not afford any entanglements now. And she knew, with a deep, piercing realization that was almost pain, that she had fallen in love with him.

It was foolish. It didn't work like this in her world, where reason ruled and life moved according to plan. And none of that mattered at all.

Lisa went up on tiptoe, her lips melting into his, turning his brief kiss into a long, slow, deliciously heated one. By the time it ended, neither one of them was breathing steadily. Quinn looked down at her for a long moment.

Then he bent his head, his arms sliding around her, and pulled her into him for another kiss. Passion swept through them, demanding, unstoppable. They kissed again and again, as if they could not get enough of each other, their bodies pressed together, yearning. They moved slowly, blindly, across the room, their hands searching and caressing, frustrated by the clothes that thwarted them.

They skirted a chair and reeled up against the wall, his strong arms around her protecting her from the impact. Lisa wrapped her arms around Quinn's neck, pressing her body up into him, moving her hips in a slow, primal rhythm that sent his desire skyrocketing. With a low groan of frustration, Quinn pulled back and glanced around. He saw the doorway just to their right and beyond it the hallway leading into her bedroom.

With a swift gesture, he bent and lifted her up into his arms and carried her down the hall to the bedroom. Lisa leaned against Quinn's shoulder, breathing in the scent of him, luxuriating in the feel of his firm muscles and the heat of his body beneath his shirt. She unbuttoned the top button of his shirt and slipped her hand beneath the material, caressing his flesh. Quinn let out a soft noise of pleasure and stopped just inside the bedroom to take her mouth in a long, passionate kiss.

At last he lifted his head and set her down on her feet. He looked down into her eyes as his fingers went to the top buttons of her blouse. His eyes never leaving hers, he worked his way down the front of her blouse, unfastening each button, then pushing her tailored white blouse back off her shoulders and down her arms. He went next to the fastening of her skirt, but Lisa, smiling, shook her head.

"Oh, no. Turn about," she told him and set about unbuttoning and removing Quinn's shirt.

He smiled, his eyes hot with desire, as she exposed his chest and caressed its wide expanse. The whole time, he kept his hands lightly on her waist, his thumbs caressing her skin. When Lisa leaned forward and pressed her lips against the hard center line of his chest, he sucked in his breath and his fingers dug into her waist. Lisa, smiling against his skin, trailed kisses across his chest, going up on tiptoe to reach as high as she could. Then her lips made their way across his chest and settled on one flat masculine nipple, pulling the little bud into her mouth and suckling it.

Quinn groaned, his heart pounding against his chest, and his hand slid up her sides and came around to cup her breasts. He caressed her breasts through the material of her bra, his thumbs caressing and exciting the hard buttons of her nipples as her mouth caressed his. His fingers fumbled at the fastening of her bra, undoing it and pulling it off. He stepped back a little to look down at her breasts as he cupped their fullness in his hands. His face was slack with passion and his chest rose and fell in swift pants.

"You are so beautiful," he murmured. He squeezed her breasts gently and his thumbs moved over the nipples, watching as they tightened in pleasure.

He bent and lifted her, his arms beneath her buttocks, so that his mouth could feast on her breasts. He pulled the pink-brown nipple into his mouth, sucking and teasing it with his tongue, lashing it gently into an ever-harder state. Lisa sucked in her breath, her fingers digging into his shoulders, awash in desire. Moisture pooled between her legs as the throbbing there grew stronger and stronger.

Her hands moved up and dug into his short, crisp hair as she whimpered with almost unbearable pleasure. She felt as if she would explode if he did not stop, yet she wanted him to go on forever.

''Quinn...please...''

His only answer was to walk the few feet to her bed and lay her down upon it. He unfastened her skirt and pulled it off, then stood looking down at her, his eyes ablaze. Slowly he caressed her flesh, running his hands down her chest and stomach, then over her thighs, first outside, then in, moving up to the heated juncture of her legs. He teased them both by stopping before he reached the center of her desire and sliding his hands back down her thighs and around, slipping up the back of her legs and under the flimsy material of her panties to the soft mounds of her buttocks. He dug his fingers into the fleshy curves, lifting her hips from the bed.

Lisa groaned, circling her hips enticingly. His smile was part pleasure, part pain, as he moved his hands down her thighs again and then back up the inside of her legs. But this time he did not stop short of his goal, but cupped her sex in his hand, feeling her heat through the thin material of her underwear. He rubbed his fingers gently against her, eliciting a choked groan from Lisa. She dug her heels into the bed and arched up against his hand. She felt on fire, her entire being seemingly focused where his hand touched.

Roughly, Quinn hooked his hands in the sides of her panties and pulled them down, tossing them aside. Just as impatiently he shucked off his own trousers and underwear, revealing a body that was as fully magnificent as Lisa had imagined it. He stretched out on the bed beside her and devoted himself to exploring her body. He kissed his way down her chest and over her breasts, fastening at last on her nipples and arousing them to hard, dark points. As he suckled at them, his hand slid down her body and in between her legs, opening and caressing her. Deftly his fingers delved into the hot, slick folds of her femininity, stroking and pressing until Lisa quivered with arousal.

Never in her life had she felt such pleasure, and she thought with each new surge of excitement that soon she must explode, but Quinn expertly stoked the desire in her to further and further heights without sending her over the edge. She whimpered and twisted, her fingers digging into his back. Quinn's own breath was ragged and tortured.

At last, when Lisa thought that she could stand it no more, Quinn moved between her legs and came inside her, thrusting deep with exquisite slowness. He moved, and she matched his rhythm, lost in a haze of pleasure. They were so close, so entwined that she could hardly tell where she left off and he began, and for the first time she understood what it meant to be one. This was love. This was true union. And when at last the desire exploded deep inside her and Quinn shuddered, wrapping his arms around her, the two of them lost in their passion, she knew that something inside her had changed. She would never be the same again.

Lisa awoke before her alarm the next morning, hazily aware of a heavy weight across her chest. Her eyes fluttered open, and she gradually realized that the weight was a man's arm thrown over her. *Quinn.* The memory of the night before came back in a rush, and she turned her head to look at Quinn. He was still sound asleep, face peaceful in repose. The sunlight through the window backlit his hair, turning it into fiery spikes.

She smiled, easing out from under his arm and turning on her side to gaze at him. Her heart fell full almost to bursting, and she was sure that there was a sappy grin upon her face. *How could it make her so happy just to look at this man asleep in her bed? And what was she going to do when it came time to leave?*

Pain pierced her at the thought, and she wondered, with a clutch of panic, if she had been wrong to let things go so far last night. Yet she knew that she would not have given up what she had experienced for anything. Even if it meant sorrow and loss in the future, their lovemaking had been something to treasure.

Quinn's eyes flew open, and he was instantly alert. Then he smiled, his body relaxing. "Hey, darlin'."

"Hey, yourself."

He reached up and smoothed his forefinger over her forehead. "What's the frown about? You unhappy? Regretting it?"

"No. I don't regret it at all," Lisa replied honestly. "I-it was the best night of my life."

His smile grew wider. He raised up on his elbow, leaning over to kiss her lightly on the lips. "Well, there'll be plenty more, I promise you. So why the worried face?"

Lisa shrugged. "Just thinking…about when I leave."

"Leave?" Now it was he who frowned. "What are you talking about? Are you going somewhere?"

"Back to Dallas, eventually. I'm only here for a year."

"A year! Hell, darlin', that's a long time away. No need to worry about that."

Lisa smiled faintly. "I suppose not." She certainly wasn't going to tell him that she worried about it because she had fallen in love with him. *That* would be guaranteed to scare a man off.

"Right now," he went on, brushing his knuckles against her cheek, "let's just concentrate on this…."

He kissed her again, this time long and lingeringly.

When at last he pulled back, Lisa let out a small sigh of contentment. "All right," she said happily and went back into his arms.

* * *

For the next two weeks, Lisa drifted in a world of joyous romance. Every moment with Quinn seemed magical. She went to work smiling, much to the amusement and satisfaction of her secretary, who reminded her that she had told her from the beginning that she should date Quinn. Neither clients nor long-winded colleagues nor even hardheaded prosecutors could destroy her mood. Everything in the world seemed different—brighter, sharper, more wonderful.

She put out of her head all thoughts of the future. She refused to think about what would happen when the time came for her to leave Hammond and Angel Eye. Instead, she resolved, she would simply enjoy life as it was. She would revel in the storybook days she spent with Quinn.

She spent every evening after work with him, sometimes going out for dinner or a movie, but more often just spending the time alone together at her apartment or Quinn's house. They cooked dinner together, laughing over their mistakes, then sat on the couch, talking or watching TV, spending their time in ordinary ways. But the feeling inside, the atmosphere around them, was anything but ordinary. Desire sizzled between them with merely a look. His fingers linked through hers brought a sweet bliss. Watching him cross the room sent a thrill through her.

Lisa told herself that she was being silly. This sort of romantic fizz was not the kind of thing she felt. She was a steady person, the kind with her feet firmly planted on the ground. But such reminders didn't make a dent in her mood. She was in love, and for the first time she understood how little practicality mattered when one loved.

She retained enough common sense not to tell Quinn of her newfound feelings. She wasn't about to risk anything spoiling what they had.

Even their jobs intruded only peripherally. She heard nothing from Benny, and Quinn did not call him in for questioning again. Quinn did not mention the case involving the body they had found in the field except for an occasional grumble that INS or the DEA were poking their noses into it.

Then, one night, Quinn's cell phone went off shrilly in the middle of the night, startling Lisa awake. She sat up, heart pounding, at first unsure what had happened. Quinn was already halfway across the room, grabbing up his phone and answering it with a terse, "Yeah?"

He listened, frowning. Lisa sat up, a sense of dread settling over her. She reached out and turned on the lamp on the nightside table, blinking in its sudden glare. Quinn listened, replying periodically in sharp terse words: "When?" "Where?" "Who's on it?" "I'll be right there."

He hung up and quickly began to dress.

"What's the matter? What is it?" Lisa asked.

He glanced at her. "Sorry. I've got to go." He paused, then added in a flat voice, "There's another body."

Chapter 10

"What?" Lisa gaped at him. "A—a murder?"

He nodded shortly. "Yep. No question this time. This one was shot in the head."

Lisa watched, stunned into silence, as Quinn finished dressing. He came over to the bed and kissed her briefly, almost absently, on the forehead. Then, sticking his phone in his back pocket and grabbing up his keys, he was gone.

She sat as she was for a while, knees pulled up and her arms wrapped around them, gazing into nothingness. It was difficult to absorb that murder had happened again in this quiet place. The first one had been bad enough, someone callously abandoning a body in an empty field, but at least the death had been the result of an accident. This, however, was clearly intentional.

Lisa shivered and got up. She knew she would not be able to go back to sleep this night. She glanced at the clock beside her bed. *Four o'clock.* She decided to put some coffee on to brew and get to work on the papers she had brought home last night and then had not even looked at. Padding into the kitchen, she pulled out the coffee and began to measure it into the coffeemaker.

Her thoughts, however, were on Quinn and what he had gone to do. *Was this murder connected to the other body they had found?* It seemed too coincidental for it not to be. Two suspicious deaths probably exceeded the total in a town like Angel Eye for several years. With a clutch of dread in her stomach, she wondered if Benny were somehow connected with it. He had vehemently denied recognizing the other corpse, and Lisa believed him. She was not so certain, however, that he was not involved in whatever illegal activity was going on. He had been shaken and scared that day at the sheriff's office, and she suspected that there was more reason for it than just seeing the picture of a body.

She sincerely hoped that he was not involved in it. She liked Benny and hated to think that he had gotten caught up in anything illegal, but especially in something as dangerous as drug-smuggling.

Later that morning when she went into work, the office was already buzzing with gossip about the body found outside of Angel Eye the night before.

"I heard he'd been there for a long time," her secretary Kiki said, looking at Lisa for confirmation.

Lisa shrugged. "I don't know any more than you do. Probably less."

The girl gave her a disbelieving look. "Right. You and Quinn are…"

"Just because I've gone out with Quinn doesn't mean that he calls me first thing about dead bodies," Lisa retorted.

Kiki shrugged. "Well, that's what I heard. That the body was in pretty bad shape, but there was ID this time. Don't know who it was, though. Some kids who were out parking found it. Gross. Can you imagine, going out to some secluded spot to fool around and coming on a decomposing corpse?"

Lisa made a face. "That's gross all right. I don't think I want to hear any more of the details."

"That's all I know," Kiki admitted.

Lisa heard about the murder wherever she went that day—the district courthouse, the burger stand where she had lunch, even the drugstore where she picked up a few purchases after she left the office that evening. It was there that she learned that the radio had announced the identity of the body—a young man from San Antonio named Miguel Sanchez. Lisa breathed a sigh of relief, realizing what she had not admitted to herself earlier—that there had been a bit of fear in the back of her mind that the body might turn out to be Benny Hernandez.

She did not hear from Quinn until almost seven o'clock, when he called her apartment to tell her that he had to break their date for the evening. "It looks like I'll be tied up here for hours," he said, his voice weary.

"I'm sorry. Has it been terrible?"

"Not good," he admitted. "I've seen worse, but not here. I really hate it that it's happened here."

"I know. I'm sorry." Everything Lisa could think of to say seemed inadequate. She remembered the things he had told her about his time in the San Antonio police force and how he had hoped to leave it behind him when he moved back to Angel Eye. "I heard it was somebody from San Antonio."

"Yeah. At least I didn't have to notify the parents—the San Antonio police did that. But it's still connected here. It was in a remote spot, not someplace that somebody from S.A. just looking to dump a body would have found. I think somebody local put it there."

"And you think it's connected to the other?"

"Wouldn't you?"

"Yeah."

"I may have to pull Benny in again," he warned.

"I figured as much."

She spent the rest of the evening trying to read a book. When the phone rang shortly before ten o'clock, she was not surprised to hear Benny Hernandez's voice on the other end of the line.

"Ms. Mendoza?"

"Benny. Are you at the jail?"

"No. No. I just called…I heard they found another dead guy. Is that true?"

"Yes, it is. Do you know anything about it?"

"My grandmama said—she said his name was Miguel."

"Yes. That's what I heard. He was from San Antonio."

"Okay."

"Benny, if you are somehow involved in this, it looks like it's turning into something pretty serious. Maybe we need to talk."

"No. I can't."

"You can't talk to me? Benny, I'm your attorney."

"I gotta go. I—got something I need to do."

"Benny. Don't do anything hasty. I'm here to help you. Remember that."

"Yeah. Okay. Goodbye."

"Benny—"

The dial tone buzzed in her ear. With a sigh, Lisa put the receiver down. She sat, thinking about the phone call, worrying her lower lip with her teeth. The phone call made her uneasy. There had been an undertone of fear in Benny's voice, she was sure. She wished that he had agreed to talk to her.

After a while, she got up and began to get ready for bed. The apartment felt strangely empty. It was the first time in two weeks that she had gone to bed without Quinn, she realized. It was a little shocking how quickly she had become accustomed to his presence...dependent on it, even. The thought bothered her. She had gotten along without Quinn for twenty-seven years of her life; she certainly should be able to get through one night without him.

Irritated with herself, she got into bed and tried to go to sleep. But sleep would not come. She tossed and turned, and her mind kept going to the phone. She had thought that Quinn would call her before she went to bed, just to wish her good-night. She was disappointed—and annoyed that she felt so disappointed. Was she turning into a clinging woman—unable to sleep without him there, expecting him to call her every night?

The phone rang, and she jumped for it. "Hello?"

"Hey, darlin', it's me," Quinn said on the other end of the line.

Lisa could not keep a smile from spreading across her face. "Hi, 'me.' How are you?"

"Tired," he answered candidly. "I'm about to turn in. But I didn't want to go to sleep without saying good-night to you." He paused, then said, "You know, it's damned lonely here without you."

"Here, too," Lisa replied, warmed by his words.

"I thought about coming over, but I'll be up early tomorrow morning. I'm just going to grab a few hours sleep. No point in disturbing you."

"You don't disturb me."

"Don't tempt me." He sighed. "I told Ruben I'd be here."

"Okay."

"Talking to you makes it better."

"Yeah?"

"Yeah. I'll see you tomorrow."

"Okay."

"I miss you."

"I miss you."

They stayed on the phone for a few minutes longer, both of them reluctant to hang up. But finally they said their good-nights, and Lisa went back to bed, smiling to herself.

She was dressing for work the next morning when there was a knock on her door. Surprised, she went to the door, buttoning her blouse and tucking it in as she walked. She looked through the peephole and saw Quinn standing outside.

Smiling, she undid the lock and opened the door. Quinn looked at her. His expression was grim, and she could see the lines of weariness at the corners of his eyes and mouth.

"Have you seen Benny?" he asked without preamble.

"Well. Hello and nice to see you, too."

His expression softened a trifle. "I'm sorry. I'm worried. Good morning. You look, as always, beautiful." He leaned down to kiss her on the lips. "Mmm. That improves my outlook a lot."

"Good." Lisa smiled at him. "Would you like a cup of coffee? I've just made some."

"I wouldn't turn it down."

"Come on in." Lisa turned and went into the kitchen to pour him a cup. He followed her.

"Now, what is this about Benny?" Lisa asked, turning to hand him the cup. "Have I seen him?"

"Yeah. Or heard from him?"

Lisa hesitated, and Quinn caught it immediately. "You have, haven't you?"

"Well, yes, he did call me last night."

"What did he say?"

"Now, Quinn, you know I can't tell you that. It's privileged communication."

"Damn it, Lisa, I need to find him." Quinn scowled. "This is no time for legal quibbling."

Lisa stiffened. "Attorney/client confidentiality is hardly legal quibbling. The whole system would be unworkable if I had to tell you everything my clients tell me."

"I'm not asking you for any kind of confession or anything. I just want to know where he is! Don't you care about your client in any way besides legally?"

"Yes. I do." Lisa shot back, irritated by his attitude. "I happen to like Benny, and I think that he's a decent young man. That's why I'm going to do my best to keep him from being harassed and stigmatized by you and your investigation. In case you haven't noticed, Quinn, your interests and my client's are not exactly the same."

"I am trying to help him!" Quinn burst out. "A boy has been killed, Lisa, one just about Benny's age, and he was seen leaving and entering that same house where Benny has been seen. I'm sure the smuggling is headquartered there, and Benny is in it up to his eyeballs. I am trying to get him out of it before he gets sent to prison or worse."

"You're trying to get him to confess and testify against the others, so that you will have a case."

"Is that all you think I'm interested in?" Quinn asked, his voice deadly quiet. "Making a case? You think this is just another notch on the belt for me?"

Lisa saw the anger in his still face and, behind it, lurking in his eyes, the hurt. She drew a calming breath. "No. Of course not. Look, let's both calm down. I know that you are concerned for Benny. And that you care about that poor boy who was killed. But you act as if I am trying to hurt him. I'm not. I have a duty to give him the best legal protection I can. And I would not be doing that if I ignored one of the basic tenets of the law. What kind of lawyer would I be if I broke client confidentiality just because I like you and trust you?"

"Benny could be in danger. Miguel Sanchez was in and out of that house, just like Benny. I'm guessing that either there's some sort of drug war going on between them and another gang or within this gang. Or the drug ring decided for some reason that this kid was a liability. What if they decide that Benny is a liability to them, too?"

"Let me point out that if that is true, if this young man's confederates are the ones who killed him, then every time you pull Benny in, you are endangering him. What if it makes them suspicious? What if they decide that Benny broke down and confessed something to you?"

"You think that doesn't worry me?" he asked. "But I want to give Benny a chance to get out of this. And I have to solve the case. I can't let these crimes continue. You say you have a duty to Benny.

But I have a duty to the people of this county. I have to stop this, and I think Benny is my best chance of doing so. And you know as well as I that if Benny would just tell me what's going on, turn state's evidence, I could take him into protective custody so that the others can't hurt him. You can make a deal for him with the prosecutor, and he could come out with little to no time.''

"*If* he is involved and if that's in Benny's best interests, then I will do so,'' Lisa replied. "But it's my client's decision. Are you making him an offer?''

"I can't guarantee him anything,'' Quinn replied tersely. "That's for the D.A. to decide. But if he can blow this case open, as I suspect he can, then I'm sure Keith Cavanaugh will deal with him. We can't do anything for him, though, unless he tells us what's going on. And I sure as hell can't put him anyplace safe until I can find him! I have to know where he is!''

"I don't know where he is,'' Lisa replied honestly. "He did call me last night. But he didn't tell me where he was. Is he not at his grandmother's house?''

"No. That's the first place I looked. I went there last night, and Mrs. Fuentes said she would call me as soon as she heard from him. This morning, before I could even go over there again, she called me. She was worried because Benny never came home last night. We've checked out his friends' houses. We have a twenty-four-hour watch on Mr. Rodriguez's house, but it's been extremely quiet. Hardly anyone in or out for the last couple of days. I think they've pulled out of there because we're onto it. I don't know if Benny's hiding or on the run or...if something's happened to him, too."

A chill ran through Lisa and she remembered her uneasy feeling the night before when she talked to Benny. "Well, he called me in the evening yesterday, about ten, I'd say. I think he was all right then. But he didn't say anything about where he was or where he was going. It was very brief. I did tell him that I thought it was pretty serious and asked him to come meet with me, but he didn't agree to." She shrugged. "That's all I know. If he calls me again, I'll tell him what you said about the D.A. being willing to deal with him. I can't guarantee anything."

"I know." Quinn sighed and set his cup of coffee down on the counter, untouched. "I'm sorry if I jumped on you a while ago. I know you have Benny's interests at heart. I'm just on edge—"

"I understand." Lisa went to him and put her arms around his waist, leaning her head against his chest. It bothered her that they had argued again about Benny. It seemed as if at the first sign of conflict in their jobs, the idyllic closeness between them the last two weeks had just flown out the window. Had she been fooling herself that she could have everything— her job *and* a life with Quinn?

Quinn gave her a squeeze and planted a kiss on the top of her head. "I better go now. I have a meeting at eight with some guys from the DPS. The newspaper in San Antonio ran a story about Miguel Sanchez and the first body, and now everybody wants to help. It'll be a madhouse here pretty soon if I can't head some of them off.''

''Okay.'' Lisa smiled at him, and he kissed her briefly, then left.

She stood at the door after she had closed it. She felt uneasy…about Quinn…about Benny. She wished that Benny had agreed to meet her last night. She thought back over their conversation. She wasn't sure exactly why he had called. He had asked her about the identity of the murdered young man—but had that really been the only purpose for his call? His grandmother had already told him about it, and the news was all over town. He could have gotten confirmation from anyone. He had sounded nervous, and she suspected that he had called to tell her something or ask her something and then had backed off, afraid.

Apparently he had run away or gone into hiding locally. Who was he hiding from? Was it the sheriff, who was obviously looking for him? Or had he been afraid of someone else? Lisa wondered if he was already in hiding when he called her or if he had left afterward. But she had an idea about where Benny might have gone.

She felt guilty about not telling Quinn about her hunch, but she could scarcely turn her own client over to him—and, anyway, it was only a guess. Perhaps later she would check it out herself…if she was right, then she could tell Benny what Quinn had told her.

Lisa finished dressing and went to work, where the office was once again abuzz with the subject of the murdered young man. Lisa went to her office and settled down with a stack of cases that she had been neglecting recently. It took a little effort, but after a while, she was able to shut both Quinn and Benny out of her mind—at least for several minutes at a time.

An hour or two after lunch—a half-tasted sandwich eaten at her desk—there was a knock on her door.

Surprised, Lisa lifted her head. "Come in."

Her secretary opened the door and stuck her head inside. "There's a Mr. Garza out here to see you. He doesn't have an appointment."

"Garza?" It was a common name, but it didn't ring any bells.

"Enrique Garza."

"Oh!" That was the name of the man who had hired her to represent Benny. Lisa's stomach tightened nervously. If Quinn was right, he was involved in a crime ring and possibly murder. "Uh…all right, send him in."

After all, she reminded herself, what could the man do here in her office when her secretary and who knows how many other people had seen him come in? She rose to her feet as he walked in the door. He was dressed in designer slacks and a silk shirt, casual but expensive, as his clothes had been the other time she'd met him—and looking nothing at all like anyone from Hammond or Angel Eye. She put a smile on her face as she motioned toward the chair in front of her desk.

"Mr. Garza. Can I help you?"

Garza smiled thinly. "I hope so, Miss Mendoza. I am looking for Benny Hernandez."

"Oh?" Lisa kept her expression mildly curious, hoping that she did not betray the fact that her nerves had started jumping wildly at his question. "I'm sorry, but he is not here, as you can see."

"Yeah. I didn't figure he was. I was thinking, though, you might have heard from him…since you're his attorney."

"No. I haven't heard from him in some time," Lisa lied coolly. "Is there some reason why I should?"

He shrugged. "No. I thought maybe he was in trouble. Nobody can find him. So I thought maybe he would have called you."

"I see." Lisa looked at him for a moment. "I'm sorry that I can't be of more help. Have you tried his house?"

"Yeah. And his friends. Nobody's seen him." He paused for a moment, then said, "What's going on with his case? I know that sheriff hauled him in again."

"Yes, but as you no doubt know, he released him again."

"Does he have anything on the kid?"

"Mr. Garza, I really can't discuss my client or his case with you. I realize that you hired me to represent Mr. Hernandez, but Mr. Hernandez is the one who is my client, no matter who is paying the bills. I am sure that you will understand that I cannot divulge anything to you. That's privileged information."

Garza sat for a moment, regarding her with his flat, dark eyes. His gaze unnerved her, but she was careful not to shift or twitch or in any other way reveal that fact.

"So are you saying you wouldn't tell me where he is if you knew?" he asked finally.

"Not without obtaining my client's permission first," Lisa responded. "However, since I don't know where he is, it's a moot point."

"Yeah. Right." He rose smoothly to his feet and started toward the door, then turned back. "You know, Miss Mendoza, you should watch who you hang out with. You're spending a lot of time with that sheriff. Doesn't seem like a good idea."

There was something chilling about the look in his eyes as they focused on her face, but Lisa was too angered by his words to let that stop her. "I beg your pardon?" she told him icily. "I don't think my relationship with Sheriff Sutton is any of your business—or anyone else's."

"It is if it means you favor him over your clients."

"Are you accusing me of unethical conduct?" Lisa snapped. "I can assure you that I have not done anything that would be detrimental to any of my clients, nor would I ever do so. My personal life and my law practice are completely separate, and I don't allow either of them to interfere with the other."

"Well, that's good," he replied, unaffected by her outrage. "I hope you make sure it stays that way."

He turned and walked out of the office. As soon as the door was shut, Lisa flopped down in her chair. Her stomach was churning and her knees were weak. She wasn't sure whether she was more mad or scared. She wished she knew exactly how deeply Benny was involved in this. Benny was not a bad kid. Lisa was sure of that. But he could easily have gotten into something over his head.

She stood up and walked over to the window, leaning against the wall and looking out at the tangle of branches outside her window. In summer the leaves of the tree shaded her window and cooled the office, blocking the view. But now, in October, the leaves had been drifting to the ground, so that the branches were bare in patches, and she could see through them. As she looked out idly, thinking, she saw the form of Enrique Garza walk down the sidewalk away from her building. She watched as he crossed the street and continued on the other side, stopping beside a dark blue Mercedes, as sleek and expensive as his clothes.

She watched as he opened the driver's door and got into his car. But the car did not pull out from the curb. Instead, she saw the side windows slide down, and still the car sat in its place. Without thinking, Lisa slid farther to the side of the window, so that her body was not visible through the window. She waited, and so did Enrique Garza.

Lisa realized that he was not going to leave. A little frisson of fear ran through her. Garza was keeping a watch on her.

Chapter 11

Lisa moved away from the window, going instinctively to the phone to dial Quinn's number. But she stopped, her hand on the receiver. No. She couldn't call Quinn about this. He would come over and roust Garza out, and that would accomplish nothing except to convince Garza that she was in league with the sheriff. Besides, she couldn't go running to Quinn with all her problems, like a helpless female. She had a client who was in all likelihood in trouble, and her first priority was to help him.

She sat down at her desk and picked up one of her pads, starting to doodle as she always did when she was thinking. Garza's interest was in finding Benny. Therefore, she knew, he was watching her building in the hopes that Benny would come there to seek her help—or that, if she knew where Benny was, she would leave the building and go to him, enabling Garza to follow her and find Benny.

Clearly, then, she could not follow her first instinct, which had been to act on her hunch about Benny's whereabouts. Instead, she would remain here the rest of the afternoon, giving no hint that she had a clue about where Benny was, and hope that Garza would grow bored and leave. If not, she would have to come up with a plan to throw him off before she set out to find Benny. She didn't know why Garza wanted to find Benny, but she felt sure that it was not because he wanted to help him.

Since Garza was looking for Benny, that meant that Benny was hiding from Garza as well as from the police, which must mean that Benny was afraid of him. It also meant, she thought thankfully, that the other people in the smuggling ring had not killed Benny, as the other young man had been killed, a worry that had been growing in Lisa all day. No doubt Benny had contacted her last night because he was confused and scared, but then he had not been able to bring himself to tell her about the situation.

Lisa knew that he might very well contact her again. She did not think that Benny would come to her office without calling first, but if he did, he would walk right into Garza's hands. Therefore, she had to try to prevent his coming here. She reached for her phone, then hesitated, her thoughts going back to Enrique Garza. She was being paranoid, she told herself; Garza would not have been able to put a bug on her phone—and surely Quinn wouldn't have, either. Still…she reached into her purse and pulled out her mobile digital phone. She flipped through her Rolodex until she found the number for Benny's grandmother and dialed it. From what Quinn had said, she didn't think that Señora Fuentes knew where Benny was, but the old woman could have been lying to Quinn. However much his grandmother might dislike what Benny was doing, that did not mean she would turn him over to the sheriff if he was in serious trouble.

"Señora Fuentes, this is Lisa Mendoza, your grandson Benny's attorney."

"*Si?* Do you know where Benny is? Is he there?"

"No. I don't know where he is. But if you should happen to see Benny, would you please tell him I want to help him. Tell him to call me at this number—do you have a pen and paper?"

"*Si. Un momento.*"

The old woman put down the phone and returned a minute later. "Okay."

Lisa gave her the number to her mobile phone. "Tell him to call that number, not my office number. And tell him *not* to come to my office. *Comprende?*"

"*Si, comprendo.* This is very bad, isn't it, miss?"

"I'm afraid it could be. But I want to help Benny. He needs legal advice."

After she hung up, she looked up another telephone number in the yellow pages and dialed it.

"Moonstone Café."

"Is Teresa working there today?"

"Sure. You want to talk to her?"

"Please."

She waited, and after a while a young voice came on the line. "This is Teresa."

"Teresa, this is Lisa Mendoza, Benny's attorney."

"Yes?" The girl's voice turned wary.

"I don't know whether you have seen Benny or are likely to see him, but if you do, I wanted to let him know that I would like to talk to him. But he must not come to my office. Do you understand? Could you give him that message?"

"Yes…if I see him," Teresa answered carefully.

Lisa gave the girl her mobile number and repeated her warning about coming to the office. Teresa responded that she understood, and something in her carefully noncommittal voice told Lisa that she had guessed right about where Benny had gone.

She hung up and tried to settle down to the work before her on the desk, but it was hard going. Every few minutes, she got up and edged over to the window to peek out at Garza's car. It was still there, and she assumed Garza was still in it, though from this distance it was hard to see a person inside it.

Almost an hour passed before her mobile phone rang. Lisa grabbed it. "Yes?"

"Ms. Mendoza?"

"Benny! I'm glad you called."

"Yeah. I—I don't know what to do." Benny's voice sounded young and scared. "I think I'm in trouble."

"Yes, I think you may be. We have to talk, Benny.

You need legal advice. The sheriff has been by looking for you, and so has Mr. Garza.''

She heard a whispered curse, followed by a brief silence. Then Benny said softly, "Enrique Garza? He was looking for me?''

"Yes, he came to ask me if I knew where you were. Of course, I told him I did not. But he's sitting in his car in front of my office building—that's why I said for you not to come here. Is there someplace else I could meet you?''

"I—I don't know. What if he follows you?''

"I was thinking, perhaps I could go to the café for supper. I don't think he would follow me inside—it would be too conspicuous. And he wouldn't think I was meeting you—especially if I joined a friend there.''

"Not the sheriff!'' Benny blurted out.

"No. Not the sheriff. A woman friend.''

"Okay,'' he said after a moment. "Yeah, that would probably work.''

"All right. I will go to the Moonstone sometime after work, say six or six-thirty. I don't want it to look unusual.''

"Sure. See you.''

Lisa hung up, sat for another moment, lips pursed, thinking, then looked once again in the yellow pages and dialed the number for Gallagher Realty. A receptionist answered the phone and told her cheerily that Eve Gallagher was out in the field with a client and would not be returning until well after seven. Lisa thanked her, declined to leave a message, and hung up. She sat for a long moment, looking thought-fully at her phone. The only other person she could think of to meet her at the restaurant was Meredith.

Meredith had seemed quite nice, and Lisa had liked her, but she was also much quieter and more conservative than Eve. No doubt Eve would have jumped at the chance of a mysterious meeting, but she was not so sure about Meredith. Still, she didn't have a whole lot of choice. She looked up Meredith's phone number in the telephone book and called. There was no answer, but she had an answering machine, so Lisa left a message to call her on her cell phone. Meredith had said she was a teacher, so Lisa hoped that she would come home from work before long.

Lisa returned to her work, though it was difficult to concentrate on anything. When her mobile phone rang almost an hour later, she jumped on it.

"Hello?"

"Lisa? This is Meredith Turner."

"Meredith. How are you? Thank you for calling me back. I was wondering if you might meet me for dinner tonight at the Moonstone."

"Of course. That sounds like fun."

"Great. How does six-thirty sound?"

"Sure. I'll be there."

"This may sound a little odd, but could you meet me in the parking lot in front of the café? Wait for me if I'm not there yet?" If Garza did follow her, she wanted him to see that she was having an innocuous dinner with a friend.

"Uh, sure," Meredith replied, her voice puzzled.

"I'm sorry to sound so cryptic," Lisa said, "but it's kind of important."

"It's fine. I'll look forward to seeing you at six-thirty."

Lisa spent the rest of the afternoon in a futile effort to get some work done. She felt sure that she would have to go back over everything she had done. When the clock finally edged close to five, she cleaned off her desk and picked up her purse, managing to stroll out of her office just as the secretaries in the reception area were standing up to leave.

"What's this?" her secretary asked jokingly. "You're actually leaving at five o'clock today?"

"I'm meeting someone for dinner."

"Ah-hah." Kiki looked knowing.

"Not Quinn," Lisa responded.

"Even more ah-hah."

"No, no ah-hah about it," Lisa responded with a smile. "It's just a friend."

Lisa walked down the stairs with the other two women, telling herself again that such precautions were probably not necessary. Outside, she turned toward the right, where her car was parked, not daring to glance back to the left to see if Garza's car was still there. The other two women crossed the street to Kiki's car, and Lisa waved them a cheerful goodbye.

Unlocking her car, she slipped inside and started the engine, looking into the side rear mirror. She could see the edge of the front of the blue Mercedes.

She put on her seat belt, her insides jumping nervously, and pulled out into the street. A glance in the rearview mirror told her that the Mercedes was also pulling out half a block behind her.

She drove to her apartment, making no effort to lose Garza, though she checked her mirror once or twice to see if he was still following her. When she turned into her apartment's parking lot, she saw that Garza's car drove on past. Quickly she parked and got out of her car and went up to her apartment. Obviously he was not going to pursue her to her apartment door. He was probably going to wait and watch again. But Lisa could not suppress the nerves in her stomach, and she wanted to get inside her door as quickly as possible.

Inside, she showered and changed into jeans and a casual shirt. Then, not bothering with any more makeup than a quick application of lipstick, she left her apartment and once more got into her car. She did not see Garza's car, but as she drove down the street, she glanced in her rearview mirror and saw that a dark Mercedes was almost a block behind her. Obviously she had been right to take precautions, but that fact only increased her jumpiness.

She drove to Angel Eye, deriving some satisfaction from the thought that her follower would probably be hopeful that she was going to lead him to Benny, only to be disappointed when she pulled up to the café and met someone for dinner.

It was almost exactly six-thirty when she turned into the Moonstone's parking lot. She was glad to see that Meredith was already there, standing behind her small car and chatting with a couple. Out of the corner of her eye, Lisa saw that the Mercedes had parked across the street from the café. She waved to Meredith and strolled over to her. Meredith, who had said goodbye to the couple, met Lisa halfway and greeted her.

Politely Meredith did not ask Lisa why she had asked her to meet her out front. The two women walked into the restaurant, and Teresa came forward to seat them, guiding them toward a booth in the back. Lisa scooted in on the back side, where she could keep an eye on the door. Meredith glanced back curiously at the door, then returned her gaze to Lisa.

"I'm sorry," Lisa said apologetically. "I know this must seem all cloak-and-dagger."

"A little," Meredith agreed with a smile. "But don't apologize. It's making my day much more interesting than it usually is. Just tell me that you're going to explain this all later."

"I will. I promise. I may be worrying about nothing, but…" Lisa knew deep inside she was not. "But if I'm not, then it's very serious. I think someone is trying to find one of my clients, and I'm trying to throw them off the scent."

Meredith's eyes widened. "You're being followed?"

"I think so. But I really can't tell you who or why—it's one of my cases."

"Sure. I understand," Meredith said agreeably,

opening the menu. "Are we really going to eat or what?"

"Yes, but I'm going to have to leave in a few minutes. If you could just go ahead and eat until I get back... Are you okay with that?" She continued to keep her eye on the front door, but to her relief Garza did not enter the café.

"Sure. I feel like a spy or something."

"Thanks for being such a good sport."

Teresa returned, and they placed their orders. Then she looked questioningly at Lisa. Lisa turned to Meredith.

"I'm sorry," she began.

"I know, I know. You're going to leave now. That's okay. But, remember, you owe me...."

"Big time," Lisa agreed and got up to follow Teresa.

The girl led her around to the hallway beside the kitchen. The kitchen opened off one side of the hallway, and on the other side was a closed door. Teresa knocked softly at it, and a moment later, the door opened. Elizabeth Morgan stood in the doorway, and behind her lay a room which was obviously her office.

"Come in," she said, stepping out and motioning for Lisa to enter. "I don't know what's going on, and I don't want to know," she said firmly.

"Okay."

Elizabeth left, closing the door behind her, and Lisa turned back to the room. Benny Hernandez sat on a bar stool on the other side of the room beside a file cabinet. He slid off the stool and stood awkwardly for a moment.

"All right, Benny. I think you better tell me what's going on."

"I…" Benny glanced toward the door, then walked over and turned the lock. "I don't know what to do."

He paused again, frowning and looking at Lisa.

"I'm your attorney, Benny. What you tell me is privileged information. I can't reveal it to anyone, including the cops. But I need to know the truth so I can help you. The sheriff's looking for you. Garza's looking for you. What has you on the run?"

"I knew him—the guy they found dead the other day. I didn't know that first guy. I'd never seen him before—I mean, even though the picture was gross, I knew I didn't know him. But Miguel…I've seen him over at the house a few times."

"Your house?"

"No. That house—the one…the one the sheriff was asking me about."

"So you do know the house?"

"Yeah. I—we—that's where we go, where we bring the people."

"The people? Are you talking about illegal immigrants?"

Benny nodded. "Yeah, see, Paco told me that I could make this easy money." He sighed and sat back down on the stool.

Lisa settled herself on the edge of Elizabeth's desk. "By transporting illegal aliens?"

"Yeah. It was good money—and easy. We didn't have to bring 'em across the border, see. We just drove down to the Valley and out to this place, and the people'd be there. Then we'd drive them back here and take 'em to Senor Rodriquez's house. Paco was his grandson. Paco used to live here. I went to middle school with him. His family moved to San Antonio when he was in high school. I hadn't seen him for a couple of years, and then he came back last summer. Anyway, he said he had this good deal and did I want a piece of it? I said sure. I mean, it was real easy and a lot more money than I was making busing tables here. Besides, I figured I was helping those guys out, you know. I mean, it's not really a bad thing, helping somebody get into the country. It's not like stealin' or anything, right?"

"So is Paco the one who thought this up?"

"Oh, man!" Benny looked scornful. "Paco? Paco couldn't think nothin' up. He was working for some guy back in San Antonio. I don't know who. But this Garza guy, he works for him, too. He's, like, his man, you know."

"His assistant?"

"Yeah. He's real slick."

"Yes, he is."

"But I didn't know nothin' about the drugs. None of us did. We thought we were just bringing in these guys, givin' them a break."

"What did you do with these immigrants then?"

"Just took 'em to the house." Benny shrugged. "Somebody else took them somewhere after that. I don't know, really. I never thought about it till the sheriff was asking me those questions, talkin' about those work camps and stuff.'' He frowned, looking distressed. "I never meant to do anything wrong, you know. I wouldn't have done it if I thought they were hurtin' them. And drugs—I don't want anything to do with that. That's serious sh—stuff. You know? That's what Miguel was telling Paco the other night."

"The boy who was killed."

Benny nodded. "Yeah. I saw him and Paco talking, and they were real serious, you know. And Paco, he goes, 'Hey, *ese,* you got paid good money,' and Miguel, he's saying, 'Yeah, but I never bargained for this! I knew that guy. I drove him!' He was talking about the one the sheriff showed me the picture of. Miguel had heard it was from drugs, and he was all scared about it. You could see it in his face—he was scared. So Paco's tryin' to calm him down and all, tellin' him they'll go see Garza, and Miguel can tell Garza all this. Miguel, he doesn't want to go, but Paco says he has to talk to Garza, explain how he wants out. He says Garza's the one makes the decisions."

"So what happened?"

Benny shrugged. "I don't know. I left. I didn't want to get in the middle of that. I didn't know what to do." He paused, then went on, his voice roughened, "Then Miguel turns up dead."

"You think Paco killed him?"

"Hey, it's kinda hard to think anything else,"

Benny replied honestly, turning his face away from her. "Him or Garza."

"It sounds likely," Lisa agreed.

"And I heard 'em arguing!" Benny burst out, jumping off the stool and beginning to pace around the office. "Paco knows I did. He saw me—he's gotta figure I heard it. Part of it, at least. So I lit out. I didn't know where to go. All my friends—well, they're part of it, too. Paco would go to them if he was looking for me. But I figured they didn't know about Teresa. I don't—I never talk about her. She's…different from them, you know? I met her when I was working here at the café. She's from Hammond, and she goes to school there. So I came over here and waited out back to talk to her. She let me stay in the storage room."

"That's where you've been?"

He nodded. "I sleep over there on the couch after everybody leaves. She asked Ms. Morgan, and she said it was okay. She didn't mind having somebody here to watch the place at night, anyway. I used to work here, so she knows me."

"You told Elizabeth what happened?"

"No!" He looked horrified. "I wouldn't tell her something like that. She just—Teresa made up some story about me having trouble with my family. She said my stepdad had come home, and we don't get along."

"I see."

There was a long moment of silence, then Benny

asked quietly, "What am I gonna do, Ms. Mendoza?"

"I won't lie to you, Benny. You are in a bad situation." She crossed her arms and stared at the floor for a moment. Finally she raised her head. "I think there's only one thing you can do. You have to tell the sheriff about this."

"But I can't! I can't tell him! I can't squeal on my friends. I got loyalty. I got honor. You know? You're Latina, you know how it is. Paco is my friend—I can't turn him in."

Lisa knew she had to tread carefully here. For a Latin male, loyalty to one's friends was a code that was embedded deep in his culture. Benny would look with horror upon the idea of turning in his friends even though he was afraid that they would kill him. "I understand how important those things are to you, yes. But you're afraid that they're going to kill you. What kind of loyalty does that show on their part? Is that honor?"

"No," Benny agreed slowly. "I guess not, but…"

"Look, Benny, I know it's hard for you to give information about your friends to the authorities. You feel loyalty to them, and that's good. But, you know, you have a loyalty to your family, too, to the people you love. Like your grandmother. And Teresa. Maybe you could keep Paco and Garza from killing you by running away, going to some other part of the country where they'll never find you. But you will have to leave all the people you love behind. And you don't know what will happen to them."

Benny looked up at her, paling a little, quick to catch on to what she was suggesting. "You mean you think Garza will hurt them?"

"I don't know," Lisa replied honestly. "But I think it's a possibility, if he can't get to you. If he wants to send you a message."

Benny muttered a curse, dropping his head to his hands. Lisa watched him for a moment, scrupulously examining her own conscience. She wanted to make sure that she was not being influenced by her feelings for Quinn but was doing what was best for her client.

"Benny," she said carefully. "I am your attorney. My interest in this matter is doing what's best for you. And I think this is the correct course of action for you both legally and personally. Even though your intention may have been to help people when you got into this, you can see that you've gotten into something a whole lot worse. Unfortunately, you don't have a lot of choices. You can run and leave everybody you love behind and hope that Garza never catches up with you. Or you can go to prison with the others when the authorities figure it all out, and you know the odds are they will. You don't want to go to prison, Benny. You don't want to hurt your grandmother that way. Or Teresa. And if Garza finds you, it'll be even worse than prison."

Benny nodded and said in a resigned voice, "I know."

"Or you can turn state's evidence. When Sheriff Sutton came by today asking about you, he told me that he will take you into protective custody if you'll tell him about what's going on at the house. I can make a deal with the prosecutor in return for your testimony—hopefully immunity, or at least probation. You're still a juvenile, and if you give yourself up, show good faith…I think you can come out of this pretty clean. Are you willing to do it? Shall I call the sheriff and talk to him?''

Benny sighed. "Okay. Call the sheriff."

She spent a few more minutes explaining to Benny exactly what would happen, then cautioned him to sit tight and wait for the sheriff to come pick him up. He nodded in agreement, and Lisa left the office.

Hurrying out to her table, she found Meredith placidly eating and her own dinner growing cold on the table across from Meredith. "I'm starving," she said, sliding into the booth and taking a quick bite of her food. "Do you absolutely hate me?"

"No. I am terribly intrigued, however. I never realized being a lawyer was so exciting."

"Believe me, it's not, most of the time. Now, if you'll put up with some more rude behavior from me, I have to call Quinn."

"Go ahead. You want me to have them put your dinner in a doggie bag?"

"That'd be great. You're so kind."

"No problem." Meredith got up and went to ask Teresa for a take-home container, politely leaving Lisa to make her phone call in private.

She dialed Quinn's office number, assuming that he would still be at work, and after a moment, his voice came on the line. "Hey, Lisa. I just tried to call you at your apartment."

"I'm not there. I'm with Benny."

"What?" He paused, then said, "So you did know where he was."

"No. I told you—look, there isn't time for this. The thing is, Benny wants to meet with you. He's ready to talk."

"Okay. Where are you? I'll come over and pick him up."

"Wait. Not so fast. I need a few assurances from you."

"Such as?"

"Immunity from prosecution."

"You know I can't promise that, Lisa."

"Then get the prosecutor to call me."

Quinn made a low growling noise on the other end of the line. "Let me come get you first. If you're with Benny, you're in danger, too."

"I'm fine. Call the D.A. and tell him to call me. Tell him I think Benny'll make his whole case for him—Miguel Sanchez's murder, too."

Quinn muttered a low oath. "I want you out of there, Lisa."

"I will be—as soon as I hear from Keith."

He hung up without even saying goodbye.

Meredith returned with a foam container, and Lisa gratefully put her barely eaten dinner inside. They paid their check and went outside to their cars. Lisa got into her car and pulled out of the parking lot after Meredith, turning right and heading for Hammond.

She kept an eye on the rearview mirror, and she wasn't sure whether she was more relieved or scared when the headlights of one of the cars parked across the street came on and it pulled out onto the road after her.

It unnerved her to drive along the empty highway with Garza trailing her. She reminded herself that he was following her only in the hopes that she would lead him to Benny. It was very unlikely that he would attack Benny's attorney. What purpose would it serve?

Still, she breathed a sigh of relief when she turned into her apartment building's parking lot and saw the Mercedes go on down the street past the entrance. She hurried into her apartment and, without turning on any lights, went to the front window and peered out from behind the curtain. She waited for several minutes, but she saw no sign of a car or a man entering the lot.

Her cell phone rang, and she jumped, her heart pounding. Drawing a deep breath, she pulled the phone out of her purse and answered it. It was the D.A. on the other end of the line. Though he did his best to downplay the importance of Benny's testimony, she could hear the underlying note of excitement in his voice, and their negotiations over the terms of the agreement was perfunctory.

When she hung up, she dialed Quinn's office immediately. "He's at the Moonstone."

"The restaurant?" Quinn asked in disbelief. "He's hiding out at a restaurant?"

"Well, you didn't find him, did you?" Lisa countered. "Apparently it was a pretty good place to hide. Go to the back door, okay? Elizabeth said she would let you in. I'm going to call one of my colleagues and have him meet you at the jail for Benny's questioning. I've already told Benny."

"Wait a minute. Why a colleague?"

"For one thing, this is too important to screw the case up with any allegations of unethical conduct on the part of Benny's attorney. I explained it all to Benny, and I assured him that Ray Benitez is an excellent attorney. I told Ray about the possibility this afternoon, and he's looked over my notes—"

"This afternoon? You've known where Benny was since then?"

"No. I wasn't sure where he was. I acted on a hunch and I was right."

"Why didn't you tell me? Did you know this this morning?"

"I told you, I didn't *know*. It was just a guess."

"You guessed that he was at the café?"

"I knew that Benny is interested in a girl who works there, so I contacted her. I didn't know that he had been hiding out there until this evening when he told me."

"You didn't think that this might be a good thing to tell me?"

"I had to talk to Benny first. He's my client. I couldn't just set you on him."

"He could have left town in the meantime. He

could have been killed. I—ah, hell. I'm going to go pick him up now. I'll talk to you later.''

''I can hardly wait,'' Lisa replied dryly, but her words fell on empty space, for Quinn had already hung up the phone. Lisa set the receiver down sharply.

She called Ray Benitez and told him what was going on. Then she got up and moved around the apartment, checking the locks on her windows and the door out of sheer nerves. She hated waiting here while everything was going on in Angel Eye. She wanted to be in on the questioning instead of Ray so badly she could taste it. But she knew that it was better this way; she had figured it all out this afternoon. She had not told Quinn the second reason why she had set it up for Ray to be in on the questioning—so that she could lead Enrique Garza away from Angel Eye, Benny and the sheriff taking Benny in for questioning. The longer it took Garza to find out that Benny was turning on them, the better. But she had realized as she and Quinn were squabbling about Benny that it was probably far better for Quinn not to hear about that aspect of her evening.

The rest of the evening passed with excruciating slowness. She warmed up her food from the café and tried to eat it, but she found that she was too nervous to eat. She knew it would be hopeless to attempt to work on any of her cases, so she tried to read, and when that was unsuccessful, she turned on the television. She flipped through the channels, unable to find anything she could stand to watch and just as unable to sit still. Finally, she got up and began to clean her apartment. It was something to occupy her time, and at least it did not require much thought. As she worked, her mind was still on the phone, waiting for it to ring.

Instead, close to midnight, there was a sharp rap on her door, and the unexpected sound made Lisa jump. She hurried to the front door and looked out to see Quinn, arms crossed, waiting outside.

She flung open the door, saying, "Why didn't you call? Come in."

Quinn stepped inside, and it was then that she noticed the thunderous expression on his face. "'Cause I didn't want you to hang up on me."

"Hang up—oh, I see. You're planning to make me angry?"

"I don't have to plan," he shot back, and his eyes were blazing. "What the hell were you thinking?"

"What are you talking about?"

"I'm talking about the fact that Garza accosted you in your office and he's been following you around all day, and you didn't even tell me!"

"Oh. I guess Benny must have said something."

"Yeah, he said something. He told me all about your calling this afternoon and setting up the meeting. He told me about your playing your little spy games with a guy that has probably killed at least one other person."

"I was trying to protect my client. I needed to talk to Benny. What else was I supposed to do?" Lisa retorted, fists on her hips.

"You could have called me! You could have told me that Garza was there harassing you. You—"

"He didn't harass me. He just came to my office, and we had a quiet conversation."

"During which you more or less told a killer to bug off. Right?"

"Not exactly. Besides, I didn't know he was a killer at the time."

"Why didn't you call me? Did you think I wouldn't be interested in knowing that this guy was watching your office building?"

"Yes, I knew you would be very interested. And I knew you would come charging over there and roust him out, and then he'd be out prowling around talking to Benny's friends, and he just might find out from somebody about Teresa instead of wasting his afternoon sitting outside my office."

"I could have gone to the Moonstone and picked Benny up before I got rid of Garza, and then both of you would have been safe. Instead, the two of you were just out there like targets."

"Oh, yeah, that would have been great. I make plans to meet my client and then I send the cops to pick him up there. He'd really trust me a lot after that!"

"That's not as important as your life!"

"My life was not in danger!" Lisa snapped. "Garza was watching me. He wanted me to lead him to Benny. He wasn't here to kill me. What purpose would that serve?"

"If he had known what you were going to advise

Benny to do, he'd have killed you in a second. And what if he had walked into the restaurant instead of staying outside? What if he had seen you with Benny?''

"I wouldn't have gone into the back to talk to Benny in that case. I would have stayed out there having dinner with Meredith.''

"You pulled Meredith Kramer into this, too?''

"It's not like I involved her in some sort of conspiracy. I just had dinner with her. What is the matter with you? You're acting as if I have no sense. In case you don't realize it, I don't need your approval to do what I want to do. I'm an adult. I can make my own decisions. Obviously it would come as a surprise to you, but I don't just jump off and do something without thinking. I had valid reasons for what I did, and I thought it through before I did it. Stop treating me like a child!''

"Then stop acting like one!''

Lisa narrowed her eyes. "I think it would be best if you left now.''

"I'm not going anywhere.''

She raised one eyebrow. "Oh, really?''

"Yeah, really. If you think I'm going to leave you here with that son of a bitch Garza lurking around, you're crazy.''

"As well as childish?''

"Look. I'm staying right here tonight.''

"You're not. It's my decision whether you stay here tonight, and I'm saying no. I don't need your protection. I am not a little girl. I don't know why you're ranting and raving about all this. If it had been Ray Benitez who made this deal, you'd have been ecstatic. You wouldn't have run over to yell and scream at him. You'd have said, 'Hey, thanks.'"

"Yeah, well, I'm not in love with Ray Benitez."

Lisa went perfectly still. She stared at Quinn for a long moment. "What?"

"I'm in love with you, Lisa."

Chapter 12

"Oh, my God." Lisa felt suddenly weak in the knees. "I—I—"

Quinn grinned. "Well, now I've found another way to shut you up." He came closer to her, putting his hands on her arms. "I'm sorry. I know I acted like a macho idiot. You're right. You handed me my case on a platter, and I just yelled at you. I was scared. I'm not used to feeling like that. So frightened and so completely not in control of the situation. When Benny said Garza was tailing you, it scared me so bad it was all I could do to sit there those last few minutes of the interview. I took out after that so fast the D.A. probably thinks I'm crazy. All I could think about driving over here was that Garza might have gotten tired of waiting and decided to force you to tell him where Benny was. And the more I worried, the more frightened I got, the madder it made me. So I lashed out at you instead of telling you what I should have—that you made my case and you saved Benny and everyone owes you a lot.''

He bent and pressed his lips against her hair. ''I love you, Lisa.''

Much to her astonishment, Lisa felt tears seeping from her eyes. ''Oh, Quinn…I love you, too.''

''Hey, what are you crying for?'' Quinn tipped up her chin with his forefinger. ''That's supposed to be a happy statement.''

''It is!'' Lisa protested. ''I am. I just—I don't know why I'm crying.''

''Nerves,'' Quinn pronounced. ''And I have just the answer for it.''

He kissed her hair again, then pressed his lips against her forehead. When she made no protest, his mouth moved down to brush butterfly kisses on her eyelids, her tear-dampened cheeks, her mouth… Then they were kissing fiercely, their mouths hot and hungry, all the tension and jumbled emotions of the evening rushing out in a flood of passion.

They kissed again and again, tearing off their clothes and coming together in a fast, furious storm of desire and need. There was no stoking of passion; there were no lingering, teasing caresses. There was only a driving hunger, passion at a white-hot pace, and when they reached their climax, it exploded within them with a force that left them stunned and drained.

* * *

Lisa was awakened the next morning by Quinn's kisses. He kissed her closed eyes, her brow, her cheeks, her mouth: soft, brief kisses that stirred her delightfully from sleep. She opened her eyes and smiled up into his face. He was already showered and dressed, sitting on the side of her bed.

"Brought you a cup of coffee," he told her, indicating the coffee mug which he had set down on her bedside table.

"You made coffee?" Lisa sat up, pulling the sheet up around her and leaning back against the headboard. "Mmm. I could get used to this."

"I plan for you to," Quinn replied with a smile as he reached over and picked up the mug and handed it to her. "I meant what I said last night, you know. I love you."

Lisa could feel an effervescent joy bubbling up inside her, and she could not keep from grinning. "I love you, too."

"I want to wake up with you every morning," Quinn went on. "I want to marry you."

Lisa stopped in the motion of raising the mug to her lips and stared at him. "What?"

"I know. It's kind of quick. But that's the way I am. I know what I want. I know how I feel. I want to be with you for the rest of my life."

Lisa's first feeling was one of overwhelming happiness. Being with Quinn forever sounded wonderful. But the feeling was followed an instant later by a rising panic. "But, Quinn...I...I...what about my job?"

"Your job?" Quinn looked puzzled. "That won't be a problem. I mean, we got through this case okay, didn't we? There won't be anything else as touchy as this. We talked about how we could work it out."

"No, I don't mean that. I mean—my job here is over in less than a year. I'll be going back to Dallas then."

"I'm sure they would be happy for you to stay on. That was the reason they gave out the grants, wasn't it? Because they can't get enough lawyers to move to rural areas?"

"Yeah."

"Or you could set up in private practice. You'd get enough clients."

"I know. It's not that. But I—Dallas is where I want to live. It's where I want to practice. I could probably live in some other city, I suppose, but Angel Eye… I'm a city girl, Quinn. I want the kind of practice I can have in a city. Big, important cases. I want to accomplish something. To help my people."

"You think you didn't help Benny? That wasn't important enough?" Quinn drew back, and his face became shuttered.

"Yes, of course it was important. But it's not what I do most of the time. Usually it's just landlord disputes and…" She trailed off miserably.

A moment before she had been unbelievably happy, and she had ruined it all. Now Quinn was stiff and remote. She knew what he was thinking as well as if he had said it: She, like Jennifer, was choosing her career over him. Pain stabbed through her, and she wanted to cry.

"Quinn, I'm sorry... I love you! I love you so much."

"Just not enough to stay with me."

"It's not that."

"Then what is it?"

"I'm talking about my whole life! This is a big decision. I—I can't just make it, snap, like that."

"You don't have to. Take all the time you want. I'm not going anywhere." But his words could not mask the flicker of hurt in his eyes, and he was still distant. "We'll talk about it later. I shouldn't have sprung it on you like this. Why don't you get up and get dressed? I'll follow you into work this morning. I called the office, and Garza is still at large. They rounded up Paco and a bunch of the others last night, but they can't find Garza. He may have run back to San Antonio, but I don't want to take any chances. As long as he's still at large, I'm going to escort you to work and back. And I've talked to the Hammond P.D. They'll drive by your office building periodically, just to make sure his car's not there."

Lisa felt too dispirited to argue. Besides, the fact that Garza was free made her feel uneasy. She was grateful, frankly, for Quinn's protectiveness today.

She showered and dressed quickly, not wanting to keep Quinn waiting. She felt uncomfortable, anyway—she knew she had disappointed Quinn, and she herself was in turmoil over Quinn's proposal. Everything would seem better and clearer, she thought, when she was by herself and could think the situation over.

She drove to work, Quinn following her. It struck her how quiet and peaceful the drive was, how attractive the old tree-lined streets were. Even her office building, old and squat, was shaded by spreading live oak trees and elms, planted and nurtured by former occupants.

There was no sign of the dark-blue Mercedes anywhere around her office building. Lisa gave a wave of her hand to Quinn and went inside. She went first into Ray's office to discuss the police interview with Benny last night. After that she walked down the hall to her own office and sat down behind her desk. She crossed her arms on the desk and laid her head down on them. She felt as if she wanted to cry. What was she going to do?

It frankly had not occurred to her that Quinn would ask her to marry him. She was not prepared for the warring emotions within her. She was a city girl; she had never thought of living anywhere else. It was boring here. But she had friends...

A smile touched her lips as she thought of the Monday-night visits with Elizabeth, Meredith and Eve. She remembered the fun she had had with Eve on their shopping expedition to San Antonio and how Meredith had come to her aid the day before, no questions asked. She hardly knew them, but already they were good friends. There were things to do here, parties, friendly people. Most of all, there was Quinn. She had been with him every spare moment the last two weeks, and she had been happier than she had ever been. She hadn't once thought about how she missed Dallas.

But, she reminded herself, she was in the first flush of love right now. Later, it would be different. Later she would miss the sights and sounds of the city, the restaurants and shops, the theaters and clubs. If she married Quinn, she would be condemning herself to an entire life spent in a town smaller than the graduating class of her high school.

And there was her career. It was all well and good for Quinn to be hurt that she was choosing her career over their love, but, after all, he was not offering to give up his career to be with her.

Grimacing, she shoved the thoughts aside and tried to settle down to work. It was difficult, but she stuck doggedly to it. At lunch she asked her secretary to bring her back a sandwich when Kiki returned from her own lunch. She felt a little cowardly for doing so, but she had no desire to run into Mr. Garza somewhere. She wondered if he had discovered that Benny was in jail and turning state's evidence. If so, she thought, he would surely be packing up and leaving rather than hanging around in Hammond trying to contact her.

She was standing at her filing cabinet, searching for an errant file, when she heard the sound of the door opening behind her. "Thanks, Kiki," she said without turning around. "Just put it on my desk, please."

The door closed. It was the sound of the steps

across the old wooden floor that made her turn around, for it sounded nothing like Kiki's heels.

Enrique Garza stood a few feet away from her, a large and lethal-looking automatic aimed straight at her.

Quinn hated paperwork. It was especially hard today, when his thoughts kept going back to Lisa and the way she had reacted to his marriage proposal. He had gone about it all wrong, he knew. He should not have sprung it on her like that. It was too soon in the relationship, no matter how sure he was of his own feelings.

But he kept pulling his mind back from where it strayed and returning to the stack of work that had built up the past week. When the telephone rang, it was a welcome break.

"Call for you on Line One, Sheriff," Betty said. "I know you don't want to be disturbed, but he said it was urgent. Would only speak to you."

"That's okay, Betty," Quinn said. "I'll take it."

There was a click and a moment later a male voice came on the line, "Hello, Sheriff."

The voice was oddly muffled, and the back of Quinn's neck prickled. "Yes. Who is this?"

"Someone you don't know. It's not important. What's important is the fact that you've got a certain friend of mine. And I have a certain friend of yours. I thought we could make a trade."

"What? Who? Tell me what you're talking about."

"I think you know. And if you're going to try to trace this phone, don't bother. I'm talking on her cell phone."

"Her? Who are you talking about?" Fear was settling in Quinn's stomach.

"Guess."

"Lisa? Are you telling me that you have Lisa? Who the hell are you? Garza?"

There was a low chuckle. "Man, you are full of questions. But I think you already know the answers to all of them."

"You want Benny."

"Give that man a prize."

"You think I'm actually going to give up a witness to you?"

"If you don't, the next time you see this lady, you'll hardly recognize the corpse."

Quinn closed his eyes as cold swept through him.

"How about it, man? You want to trade? Or shall I begin cutting?"

"I want to talk to Lisa. I don't believe you have her."

"Sure, man. I got nothing against that."

There was a moment's silence, then Lisa came on the phone. She was struggling to sound calm and confident, but terror laced her voice, "Quinn? I'm sorry. He just walked into my office—"

The man came back on the phone. "Convinced?"

"Yes." Quinn's mind was racing.

"So…we got a deal?"

"You know I can't turn over a prisoner to you."

"You will if you want to see this bitch again."

Quinn ground his teeth, trying to keep a hold on his temper. "Garza, be reasonable. We've already got you for drug-smuggling and murder. You really want to add kidnapping to the list?"

Garza chuckled. "I'm looking at lethal injection already, man. You think kidnapping's going to make me any deader?"

"If you turn yourself in, we might be able to work out a deal. Think about it. You know things—you can name people. You could give us ten times more than Benny. You know you could."

"I'm not stupid. They aren't going to let me walk for murder."

"The feds are interested, you know. They could take you right out of my hands. This is just a local case. You know they'd do it if they thought they could break up a big drug ring."

There was a long pause, and Quinn thought he had him, but then, with a tinge of regret, Garza replied, "Nah. Wouldn't do me much good dead. I turn, and I'll be dead years earlier than on Death Row."

"There's protection, Garza."

His answer was a snort. "Yeah, right. Make up your mind, Sheriff. You trading Benny for your woman or am I going to pull the trigger right here?"

"I'll trade!" Quinn said quickly. "You know I will. But she better not be hurt in any way, or you're a dead man."

"Yeah, yeah."

"I'll meet you in an hour."

"Oh, no. I set the time and location, not you. You think I'm going to let you get snipers in place, you're crazy."

"Snipers?" Quinn repeated in a tone of disbelief. "What do you think, I've got a SWAT team here? You're not in San Antonio now, Garza. Where'd you want to meet, then? Are you still at her office?"

"You think I'm nuts? No, we're not at her office." Garza hesitated.

Quinn guessed that he was going over the places he knew in the area. Being an outsider, he wouldn't know many.

"There's an old warehouse by the railroad tracks here in Angel Eye," Quinn suggested. "It's deserted."

"I don't want no buildings around. I told you that."

"Then how about an open field? No buildings for snipers to hide in, if I had any snipers. How about where the John Doe was dumped? Empty field. No place for anybody to hide. And you know how to get there."

"Just you and me. You don't bring nobody else. 'Cept Benny. I'll bring the girl."

"Agreed."

"But I want it now. Not in an hour."

"It'll take a while to sign him out of jail," Quinn pointed out. "You've got to give me at least half an hour."

"Half an hour. You be there or your lady friend is dead."

"I'll be there."

Lisa sat scrunched up against her side of the car. Her hands were cuffed in front of her in her lap; the key was in Garza's pocket. She glanced over at the man driving the car. Garza was tense and jittery, his fingers drumming incessantly on the steering wheel as he drove, his eyes flickering from the road to her to the rearview mirror of his car. His gun rested in his lap, within easy reach.

She did not believe for a moment that Quinn was really going to give up Benny to Garza. It had surprised her when Garza smirkingly told her that the sheriff had agreed to the deal, but then she realized that Quinn was no doubt planning some sort of trick. She knew that she had to stay alert, ready to run or drop to the ground if shooting started. She knew that she had one advantage, the same one that Quinn had with this man: Garza underestimated them, Lisa because she was a woman, and Quinn because he lived in a rural area—he had referred to Quinn contemptuously as "Deputy Dawg" more than once. She thought it likely that Garza would let his guard down with her.

Garza turned off the road onto the dirt road into the ranch. A minute later, they were rattling across the cattle guard. Garza slowed down over the bumpy cattle guard, and for an instant Lisa considered jumping out of the slow-moving car. But she knew that

her door was locked; she had seen Garza lock it with
the button on the driver's side. It would take precious
time to unlock it—if that was even possible, for she
didn't know if the car had child locks that could be
engaged from the driver's side, making it impossible
to unlock it. It would be better, she thought, to wait
until later, when Quinn was here.

The road turned into a dirt track and then disappeared altogether, and soon they were simply driving
across the field. Garza cursed at the bumps and ruts
and the effect they had on his elegant car. He stopped
well short of the middle of the field and swung his
car around to face the entry to the ranch. He stopped
the engine. They waited.

Lisa's fingers felt like ice, and her stomach was
twisted in knots. Why had she felt as if she were safe
inside her office? Why hadn't she locked her door?
She cut her eyes toward her companion. Garza was
holding his gun loosely in one hand. The fingers of
his other hand were still tapping on the steering
wheel, and circles of sweat were forming on his shirt
even in the cool fall temperature. Garza was obviously nervous. She wondered if that improved the
situation or just made it even worse.

"There!"

Garza's exclamation made Lisa jump. She looked
in the direction of the road and saw a car approaching
them across the field. Quinn was here. Her stomach
knotted even more tightly.

The sheriff's car rolled to a stop still some distance
from them. Garza's hand tightened around his gun.

The driver's door of the other car opened, and Quinn stepped out, shielded by the open door. "Garza!"

Garza pushed a button on his door and slid across the seat to Lisa. He shoved the gun into her side. "Okay. Get out now, slowly. I unlocked it. Don't try anything, like running, or you're dead. You understand?"

Lisa nodded.

"Okay. Do it."

Lisa opened the door and stepped out slowly, Garza right behind her. He held her left arm in a tight grip and pressed the barrel of the gun into her back with his other hand.

"Where's the kid?" Garza shouted at Quinn. "You think I'm kidding about shooting her?"

"No!" Quinn said quickly and jerked his head toward his car. "He's here in the back. I just gotta get him out."

"Okay. But first, take that pistol out and throw it down."

Quinn nodded and reached down to the gun on his belt. Removing it carefully, he tossed it on the ground. Then he opened the back door and ducked inside. He reemerged, pulling a wriggling, squirming figure in an orange jail jumpsuit out of the car. Benny's head was down, and he was hunched over, pulling and twisting in an attempt to get away.

"Damn it, Benny!" Quinn shouted, wrapping his long arm around the slight figure and dragging him out from the protection of the car. They started toward Lisa and Garza.

Lisa was amazed that Quinn had actually brought Benny with him. She had presumed that he was laying some sort of trap for them, that they would be encircled by his officers. Beside her Garza let out a snort of humor.

"Kid's smarter than he is. He knows how it's going to end."

Quinn pressed on, pulling Benny with him. Benny was bent over, struggling, only the top of his head visible. Lisa felt Garza tensing beside her, and the pressure of the gun on her back grew lighter. She knew that he wanted to fire now at the two men, killing both Benny and Quinn. However, he was facing a dilemma in that he had to take the gun off Lisa to do so. She would be able to run or even throw herself against him to keep him from hitting Quinn. Her first instinct was to jump on his gun arm if he tried to fire at Quinn, but if Quinn had a sniper somewhere aiming at Garza, that action would make it impossible for the sharpshooter to get Garza without risking hurting her, too. She had to trust that Quinn knew what he was doing, that he had planned this in such a way that Garza would be caught and she would be safe. Her running away at the first chance would be what would aid him then. It was strange that he had chosen to endanger Benny, but she trusted him with both their lives.

She tried not to tighten up and reveal in any way that she had felt the lessening of the pressure. She walked steadily, every sense alert, every nerve on edge. Garza half turned away, bringing the gun from behind Lisa's back and around her to fire it. As soon as she felt him move, Lisa spun away and took off running. There was the explosion of a gun firing, and instinctively she whirled, looking back at the three men.

To her astonishment, she saw that Benny had straightened and held a gun in his hand, aimed straight at Garza. Apparently it was he who had fired, for Garza was spinning and falling to the ground. She realized in the same instant that the man in the orange jumpsuit was not Benny Hernandez at all, but Ruben Padilla, Quinn's chief deputy. Quinn's plan had not been sharpshooters but a false Benny concealing a gun—and his face—by bending over at the waist in an apparent struggle.

Even as she realized what had happened, Quinn and Padilla ran toward the fallen Garza, and, seemingly from beneath the earth, two more deputies rose from behind Lisa and Garza and converged upon the fallen man. She realized then that there was a ravine hidden farther on and Quinn, not taking any chances, had also hidden a couple of sharpshooters. As he ran, Quinn reached behind him, pulling a second gun from the back of his belt. As he brought it back to his side, Garza raised up from the ground and fired. Quinn spun and fell, hit.

Lisa screamed and ran to Quinn, paying no attention to the second shot Padilla fired or to the three deputies pouncing on the criminal. Her only thought was Quinn. She cried his name over and over, dropping down on her knees beside him.

He opened his eyes and smiled at her, putting his hand up to the bullet hole in the front of his shirt. "Damn!" he murmured. "That knocked me down."

"You're not hurt?" Lisa stared at him, astonished.

His grin broadened as he sat up, shaking his head. "Kevlar vest. Padilla's got one on, too. I'm not big on taking chances."

"Oh, Quinn!" Lisa couldn't hold back the sob that surged up in her chest. "I thought you were dead!"

She flung her arms around him, and he wrapped his own around her, pulling her tightly against him. Tears poured from her eyes, and her breath came in hiccuping sobs. "I love you. Oh, thank God you're all right. I love you."

He kissed the top of her head. "I love you."

Lisa's eyes flew open. She blinked, disoriented. It was a moment before she remembered where she was. She had fallen asleep sitting on a couch in Quinn's outer office. She sat up, and a coat slid down from her shoulders. She looked at the leather jacket and realized it was a cop's jacket; Quinn had doubtless laid it over her when he saw her sleeping.

She looked across at his inner office. The door was closed. He had been closeted in there since before she fell asleep. He had been in and out with one official or the other most of the day since the shooting, his meetings broken up by a press conference and a few discussions with his employees. Lisa had spent much of her time on this couch. Though Quinn had had a number of duties that he had had to attend to, neither one of them had been willing to be separated any farther than the few feet from the couch to his office. Quinn's secretary had fussed over and cosseted her, bringing coffee and sweets and even dinner in a bag from the Moonstone. Several of the deputies had stopped by to chat and update her on the news from the hospital, where Enrique Garza had gone through surgery and was expected to recover and be able to stand trial. She had also been visited by the dispatcher and seemingly almost every employee in the county courthouse. The shootout on Red Klingman's ranch was the biggest news here in years.

Most important, every few minutes Quinn had come out to check on her, even if it was no more than to stick his head out the door and smile at her. More than once, he had come out and sat on the couch with her for a few minutes. They didn't say much; it was enough simply to sit beside each other, hands linked.

The door to his office opened and Deputy Padilla and another man came out. They nodded toward Lisa, and she smiled in return. But her attention was on Quinn, who had come out of the door after the men and locked it. He strolled across the room toward her now, and Lisa stood up to meet him.

"Hey, darlin'." He wrapped his arms around her and pulled her close. "God. I don't know how I'm going to let you out of my sight again. Think you can operate your office here?"

"It might cause a few problems," Lisa replied

with a smile. She snuggled against him with a sat-
isfied sigh.

"You ready to go home?" he asked. "I can finally
leave."

"Sure."

They drove to his house, where Jo-Jo the cat met
them with a wounded dignity that could only be as-
suaged by the immediate offering of food. Quinn fed
him, then led Lisa to the couch in the living room
and sat down. He pulled her into his arms, and she
curled up against him, her head on his chest, lulled
by his warmth and the reassuring thud of his heart-
beat.

"I've never been so scared in my life," he said
after a long moment. "When Garza told me he had
you, my heart dropped down to my feet. I don't know
what I would have done if I had lost you."

"I know. I felt the same way when I saw you get
shot. I was frozen with terror."

"I did some thinking before that, too. And then,
when I thought you might die, I knew that all that
mattered to me was being with you. I'm not pushing
you, darlin'. Don't worry—you can take all the time
you want to decide. But I thought, you know, if we
got married, when your year is up, you wouldn't
have to stay here. Maybe you could get a job in San
Antonio, and we could live halfway there. Both of
us would have a forty-five minute drive to work. Lots
of people drive that kind of distance. Or, if you want
to go back to Dallas, we could move there. I could
resign as sheriff, and I'm sure I could get a job in

Dallas. I could go back to being a cop. Or any other city you want. I don't have to live in the country."

Tears welled in Lisa's eyes, and she sat up to look at him. "Oh, Quinn…you would really do that for me?"

"Of course I would. You're more important to me than anything else."

"Thank you." Lisa leaned forward and kissed him, the tears spilling out of her eyes. Then she sat back, swiping away her tears with the back of her hand. "But I did some thinking, too. When I saw you get shot, when I thought you were dead, I knew that I didn't care about that other stuff. What does it matter where I live? I like Angel Eye. I've made good friends here and…it's easy to get used to living here. I love your house…and your cat. You know Jo-Jo wouldn't want to leave."

Quinn smiled. "Darlin', you don't have to do this."

"I know I don't have to. And I love you even more because you are willing to give up your family and this house and this town that you love so much…all just to make me happy. But I don't want to take you away from here. You belong here. And the things I have here are important. Maybe the cases aren't big discrimination suits or anything, but they're big to my clients. I'm helping people here. Getting Mrs. Ramirez's landlord to make the repairs he should is important to her. Justice is just as important in small cases as in big ones. I like what I do here. And I don't need some fancy office. I like my little office at the HLA. I like the people I've met here. It would be a good place to raise a family. And, most of all, I love you. Going through what we went through made me realize how silly my objections were. All I want is you.'' She smiled a watery smile at him.

"So you're saying you'll marry me?" Quinn asked.

"Yes." Lisa chuckled. "I'm definitely saying I'll marry you."

Quinn let out a whoop and wrapped his arms around her, pulling her to him. With a sigh of contentment, Lisa melted against him.

"I love you," she murmured, and Quinn's arms tightened around her.

"I love you."

*   *   *   *   *

SILHOUETTE® SENSATION™

AVAILABLE FROM 21ST FEBRUARY 2003

THE WAY TO YESTERDAY Sharon Sala

The unbelievable chance to live one day over again allowed Mary Ellen O'Rourke to save her husband and adorable baby girl. Now she had to keep them alive. If only she knew how...

THE DISENCHANTED DUKE Marie Ferrarella

Romancing the Crown

Bounty hunter Cara Rivers and P.I. Max Ryker were working in direct competition, but the feisty beauty was the only woman who stirred his heart. Could the undercover duke tell her his secret identity?

BREAKING THE RULES Ruth Wind

Mattie O'Neal was on the run until rugged Zeke Shephard rescued her. He claimed he was just a man for the moment, but could she persuade him to mak that moment last a lifetime?

STRATEGICALLY WED Pamela Dalton

A sting operation was the only way Maggie Bennington would marry Detective Griff Murdock. But after weeks of sharing a remote cabin with her wounded groom, would she honour her vows after all...?

THE RIGHT SIDE OF THE LAW Wendy Rosnau

Kristen Harris's memory had been stolen from her, and she needed the help o dangerously compelling Blu Dufray to find the truth about who she was. But what if her past threatened their love—and even their lives...?

TAMING JESSE JAMES RaeAnne Thayne

Trouble was Jesse Harte's business...and the new schoolteacher, Sarah McKenzie, was in trouble. He ached to protect her, but could a lady like her want a lawman with an untamed heart?

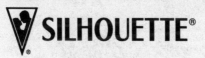

Cordina's Royal Family

NORA ROBERTS

New York Times bestselling author of
Night Tales and *Night Moves*

Available from 21st February 2003

*Available at most branches of WH Smith,
Tesco, Martins, Borders, Eason, Sainsbury's
and most good paperback bookshops.*

0303/121/SH50

SILHOUETTE® SENSATION™

presents

ROMANCING THE CROWN

The Royal family of Montebello is determined
to find their missing heir. But the search for the
prince is not without danger—or passion!

0103/SH/LC50

SILHOUETTE® SPECIAL EDITION™

proudly presents

a brand-new trilogy from

SUSAN MALLERY

DESERT ROGUES

Hidden in the desert is a place where
passions flare, seduction rules and
romantic fantasies come alive...

March 2003
THE SHEIKH AND THE RUNAWAY PRINCESS

April 2003
THE SHEIKH & THE VIRGIN PRINCESS

May 2003
THE PRINCE & THE PREGNANT PRINCESS

0203/SH/LC55

FREE!
2 Books
and a surprise gift!

We would like to take this opportunity to thank you for reading this Silhouette® book by offering you the chance to take TWO more specially selected titles from the Sensation™ series absolutely FREE! We're also making this offer to introduce you to the benefits of the Reader Service™—

- ★ FREE home delivery
- ★ FREE gifts and competitions
- ★ FREE monthly Newsletter
- ★ Books available before they're in the shops
- ★ Exclusive Reader Service discount

Accepting these FREE books and gift places you under no obligation to buy; you may cancel at any time, even after receiving your free shipment. Simply complete your details below and return the entire page to the address below. *You don't even need a stamp!*

YES! Please send me 2 free Sensation books and a surprise gift. I understand that unless you hear from me, I will receive 4 superb new titles every month for just £2.85 each, postage and packing free. I am under no obligation to purchase any books and may cancel my subscription at any time. The free books and gift will be mine to keep in any case.

S3ZEB

Ms/Mrs/Miss/Mr ....Initials ....
BLOCK CAPITALS PLEASE

Surname ....

Address ....

....

....Postcode ....

Send this whole page to:
UK: The Reader Service, FREEPOST CN81, Croydon, CR9 3WZ
EIRE: The Reader Service, PO Box 4546, Kilcock, County Kildare (stamp required)

Offer not valid to current Reader Service subscribers to this series. We reserve the right to refuse an application and applicants must be aged 18 years or over. Only one application per household. Terms and prices subject to change without notice. Offer expires 30th May 2003. As a result of this application, you may receive offers from Harlequin Mills & Boon and other carefully selected companies. If you would prefer not to share in this opportunity please write to The Data Manager at the address above.

Silhouette® is a registered trademark used under licence.
Sensation™ is being used as a trademark.